CRA
and A

JAMES PATTERSON is one of the best-known and biggest-selling writers of all time. His books have sold in excess of 325 million copies worldwide and he has been the most borrowed author in UK libraries for the past nine years in a row. He is the author of some of the most popular series of the past two decades – the Alex Cross, Women's Murder Club, Detective Michael Bennett and Private novels – and he has written many other number one bestsellers including romance novels and stand-alone thrillers.

James is passionate about encouraging children to read. Inspired by his own son who was a reluctant reader, he also writes a range of books for young readers including the Middle School, I Funny, Treasure Hunters, House of Robots, Confessions and Maximum Ride series. James is the proud sponsor of the World Book Day Award and has donated millions in grants to independent bookshops. He lives in Florida with his wife and son.

Also by James Patterson

MAXIMUM RIDE SERIES
The Angel Experiment
School's Out Forever
Saving the World and Other Extreme Sports
The Final Warning
Max
Fang
Angel
Nevermore
Forever

CONFESSIONS SERIES
Confessions of a Murder Suspect (*with Maxine Paetro*)
The Private School Murders (*with Maxine Paetro*)
The Paris Mysteries (*with Maxine Paetro*)
The Murder of an Angel (*with Maxine Paetro*)

WITCH & WIZARD SERIES
Witch & Wizard (*with Gabrielle Charbonnet*)
The Gift (*with Ned Rust*)
The Fire (*with Jill Dembowski*)
The Kiss (*with Jill Dembowski*)
The Lost (*with Emily Raymond*)

A list of more titles is printed at the back of this book

CRADLE
and ALL

JAMES
PATTERSON

1 3 5 7 9 10 8 6 4 2

Young Arrow
20 Vauxhall Bridge Road
London SW1V 2SA

Young Arrow is part of the Penguin Random House group of companies
whose addresses can be found at global.penguinrandomhouse.com

Penguin
Random House
UK

First published by Young Arrow in 2016

Cradle and All is based on an earlier James Patterson novel of the
same title published by Headline in 2000. This revised edition
includes scenes and characters from that book

www.penguin.co.uk

A CIP catalogue record for this book is available from the British Library

ISBN 9781784757199

Printed and bound by Clays Ltd, St Ives Plc

Penguin Random House is committed to a sustainable future
for our business, our readers and our planet. This book is made
from Forest Stewardship Council® certified paper

PROLOGUE

THE WOMEN'S
MEDICAL CENTER

One

Sundown had bloodied the horizon over the uneven rooftops of South Boston. Birds were perched on every roof, and they seemed to be watching the girl walking slowly below.

Kathleen Beavier made her way down a shadowy side street that was as alien to her as the surface of the moon. She hunched her shoulders and pulled up the collar on her vintage peacoat. Her black Frye boots had rubbed raw circles into her heels, but she welcomed the pain. It was a distraction from the unthinkable thing she had come to do.

This is so unreal, so impossible, she thought. *So completely insane.*

The seventeen-year-old girl paused to catch her breath at the intersection of Dorchester and Broadway. South Boston wasn't really rough anymore, not the way it used to be, but she still didn't look as if she belonged here. She was too preppy, despite the tough boots. Just a bit too pretty and golden and polished.

That was her plan, though. She'd never bump into anyone she knew in Southie.

With badly shaking hands, Kathleen pushed the tortoiseshell sunglasses she didn't need anymore back into her blond hair. She'd washed it earlier with Bumble and bumble shampoo and rinsed it with conditioner. But why, really? How ridiculous to have worried about how her damn hair would look.

She squeezed her eyes shut and uttered a long, hopeless moan of confusion and despair.

When Kathleen finally forced open her eyes, she blinked into the slashing red rays of the setting sun. Then she checked the time on her iPhone for the millionth time in the past hour.

God, no. It's already past five!

She was late for her doctor's appointment.

She started to run. She hurried past the imposing brick face of St. Augustine's parish church, past a neon-lit dive bar and a dusty florist's shop. A man on a motorcycle called out, "Blondie, what's the rush? Can I get a smile?"

She whipped herself forward, as she often did to protect herself against the New England winter. Tears ran down her cheeks, warm trails that soon turned cold.

Hurry, hurry. You have to do this terrible thing. You've come this far.

It was already twenty after the hour when she finally found what she was looking for. The gray brick building was wedged in between a twenty-four-hour laundromat and a diner with steamed-up windows.

This is the place. This . . . hellhole.

The walls were smeared with lipstick-red and black graffiti: *Abortion = Murder. Abortion Is the Unforgivable Sin.* There was a glass door and beside it a tarnished brass plaque: WOMEN'S MEDICAL CENTER, it read.

Sorrow washed over her and she felt faint. She didn't want to go through with it. She wasn't sure she could.

But she made herself walk through the front door. Inside, the reception room was calming, almost reassuring. Pastel-colored plastic chairs ringed the perimeter, and posters of sweet-faced mothers and chubby babies hung on the walls. Best of all, no one was here.

Kathleen took a clipboard left out on a countertop. A sign instructed her to fill out the form as best she could.

She sat in a powder-blue chair and began writing down her medical history in block letters. Her hands were shaking harder now. Her foot wouldn't stop tapping.

What is the reason for today's visit? the form asked.

Kathleen probed her memory for something—anything—that would help her make sense of her situation. She came up with nothing.

This can't be happening to me, she thought. *I shouldn't be in the Women's Medical Center.*

She'd made out with guys, but damn it, damn it, *damn it,* she knew the difference between kissing and...fucking.

She'd never gone all the way with anyone. She hadn't wanted to.

Not that she'd signed a purity pledge or anything like that. She just...hadn't found someone she liked enough. Trusted enough. Did that make her a prude? No, it made her *discerning.*

She'd never even let a guy touch her down there.

The tests must have been wrong, because it wasn't physically possible for them to be right. Like her dad always said, Kathleen Beavier was a good kid, the best. She was popular. She was everybody's friend.

She was a virgin.

But she was pregnant.

Two

A sudden wave of nausea came over Kathleen and nearly knocked her to the floor. She felt dizzy and thought she might throw up in the waiting room.

"Get yourself together," she said softly. *You're not the first one to go through this kind of thing. You won't be the last, either.*

She glanced at the clock over the vacant reception desk. It was nearly six. Where was the receptionist? More important, where was the doctor?

Kathleen wanted to turn around and run out of the women's clinic, but she fought off the powerful instinct. But where *was* everybody?

"You can do this," she said between clenched teeth. "No time like the present."

Kathleen stood and walked to a pinewood door behind the reception desk. She took a deep breath, possibly the deepest of her life. She turned the metal handle, and the door opened.

She heard a soft, mellow voice coming from down the hall. *Thank God, someone's here after all.*

She followed the sound.

"Hello," Kathleen called out tentatively. "Hello? Anybody? I'm Kathleen Beavier. I have an appointment."

The door at the far end of the hall was partially open, and Kathleen heard the pleasing voice inside. She slowly pushed the door open all the way.

"Hello?"

Something was wrong—she sensed it instantly. Kathleen felt she should leave, *right now,* but it had taken so much courage to come here in the first place.

The air seemed thick, almost viscous. There was a smell of alcohol. But something else, too—something metallic and heavy. Kathleen put her hand to her mouth.

It took her a few seconds to take in the full horror of what she saw.

A young, dark-haired woman was hanging from a hook high up on the wall. She wore a white medical coat. Her name tag read DR. HIGGINS. A cord was slipknotted tightly around her neck.

Her once pretty face was a brutal dark red, and her eyes were frozen open in fear. Her brown hair cascaded over her shoulders.

Trembling, Kathleen reached out and touched the woman's hand. It was still warm.

Dr. Higgins. Her doctor.

In a panic, Kathleen jerked her arm away. She wanted to run, but some force held her there. Something so powerful. So awful.

She saw a stethoscope coiled beside a pad of paper. On the pad was written Kathleen's name. Her stomach twisted. Fear and guilt and shame overpowered her in one sickening, wrenching ache.

The idea that came to her next was so strange, so overwhelming, it was almost as if it weren't her own.

Enough, she thought. *I have had enough.*

A tray of instruments glittered near the pad of paper. Kathleen took up a sharp blade. It was ice-cold and menacing in her hand.

She heard a voice—but no one was there. The Voice was deep, commanding. *You know what you have to do, Kathleen. We've talked about it. Go ahead, now. It's the right thing.*

She didn't question it. In the space between the pink sleeve of her Kate Spade oxford shirt and the crease of her left wrist, she sliced. The skin parted.

See how easy it is, Kathleen? It's nothing, really. Just the natural order of things.

Blood welled up and fell in large drops onto the floor. Tears flowed from her eyes, mixing with the blood.

One more cut. Just to be sure.

The second cut was harder for her to do. Her pretty gold cuff bracelet covered the best place on her vein, and her left hand was already weak.

She sliced into the vein again.

She sank to her knees, as if in prayer.

Kathleen managed a third slash before everything jumped to black.

She fell unconscious beneath the feet of the hanging doctor, whose mouth now seemed curved in a knowing smile.

BOOK 1
THE INVESTIGATORS

Given everything that happened, it isn't too much of a stretch to say that this is one of the most incredible stories ever, and the strangest I've ever encountered. The weirdest thing of all is that I'm part of it. A big part.

I remember how it began as if it were just moments ago.

I was sitting in my small, cluttered, but comfortable office in the Back Bay section of Boston, staring out the window toward the Hancock and Prudential towers. My day was almost over, and I was bracing myself for the hectic rush-hour commute home. Then the door opened without so much as a tap, and an elderly man stepped inside. With his gray pinstriped suit, crisp white shirt, and dark-blue silk tie, he looked like a Beacon Hill lawyer on his way to the Harvard Club.

He wasn't, though: he was John Cardinal Rooney of the Archdiocese of Boston. Besides being one of the most important religious leaders in the world, he was also a friend of mine.

"Hello, Anne, it's good to see you," he said gently. "Even under the circumstances."

"Nice to be seen, Eminence," I said, and I smiled as I rose from my seat. "But *what* circumstances? Are they the reason for...?" I gestured to his outfit. I'd never seen him in anything but a priest's robes.

Rooney nodded. "I'm traveling incognito. Because of the *circumstances*."

"I see. Well, the power suit looks excellent on you. Come in. Please, sit. It's nearly six. Can I offer you something to drink, Eminence?"

"'John' will do for tonight, my dear. Scotch if you have it. An old man's drink for an old man. And getting older in a hurry."

Aren't we all? I almost joked. But then I stopped myself, because the cardinal, at seventy, was three times my age.

I fixed him a scotch on the rocks, then got a beer out of the minifridge for myself.

I handed him his glass, smiling. "Here's to—the circumstances of your visit," I said, raising my beer.

"The perfect toast," Rooney said. He took a sip of his drink.

I had a rather complicated history with the Archdiocese of Boston, but most recently, I'd worked with certain members as a private investigator. One case involved a teacher in Andover who'd been raped by a priest who taught at the same high school. Another concerned a fifteen-year-old boy who'd shot another boy in their church. None of the cases were happy experiences for either the cardinal or me.

"Do you believe in God, Anne?" Rooney asked as he sat back in one of my soft, slightly tattered armchairs.

It was an odd question to ask me now, I thought. "Yes, I do," I said slowly. "In my own way."

"Do you believe in God the Father, Jesus, and the Blessed Mother?" the cardinal went on. He was making this strange meeting even stranger.

I blinked a few times. "Yes. In my way."

Cardinal Rooney nodded gravely. "As a private investigator," he said, "are you licensed to carry a gun?"

And now things get even stranger still, I thought.

I opened my desk drawer and showed him my Smith & Wesson Bodyguard .380. I didn't tell him that in my three years as a PI, I had never fired it.

"You're hired," he said, and knocked back the rest of his drink. "Can you leave for Los Angeles tonight? There's something there I think you should see."

2

I'll never forget Los Angeles—what I found there, what I felt there.

I'd seen graphic pictures of the epidemic on every TV network. I had watched in horror as the children of Los Angeles descended upon Cedars-Sinai Medical Center by the carload, all with aching joints and high fevers, symptoms that could kill within days.

When I arrived at Cedars, the scene was even more intense than I could have imagined. It was terrible to be there in the midst of the suffering. I wanted to turn away from it all, and maybe I should have. If I'd run into the Hollywood Hills and never come out, my life would look a lot different now.

The fabled hospital had been plunged into a confused mess. The halls rung with the sound of chaos and fear: the shouts of the emergency room nurses and doctors, the wailing of their young patients, and the sobs of the desperate parents.

We'd been warned so many times about the possibility of a

global pandemic. But so far this unexplained disease was affecting only the children of Los Angeles and a few other major cities. It was focused and ominous. Was it a portent of the future?

A curly-haired boy of four or so, wearing yellow PJs, was waiting to be intubated. I winked at him, and he managed to wink back. On another table, a teenage girl was curled in a fetal position around her stuffed sandy-colored bear. She was crying deep, heartrending sobs as doctors tried to straighten her contorted limbs. Other children were stationed along the perimeter of the waiting room. Policemen, their radios squawking loudly, manned the doorways as best they could. They restrained frenzied parents from their screaming babies. The long linoleum hallways were packed wall to wall with feverish children tossing and turning on blankets laid across the bare floor.

Each room off the main ER corridor had been turned into a dormitory of tragically sick kids. Their families seemed eerily related by the flimsy blue paper gowns and masks they all wore.

Each new image was indelibly stamped onto my mind, and then onto my soul.

The doctor walking beside me was Lewis Lavine, the hospital's director of pediatrics. He was tall and gawky, with a Conanesque pompadour. He was a rock in a sea of chaos, giving me a tour of his wards when clearly he had no time for it.

Sometimes I had to stop and make myself take deep, calming breaths. "It's even worse here than in Boston," I told him.

The same mysterious plague had just broken out before I left. I'd seen the devastation at St. Catherine's, a large hospital run by the Church. And now the archdiocese had sent me to L.A. to investigate the connection.

"It's the same disease, right?" I asked Lavine as we walked hurriedly down the hall.

15

"Yes, of course," he said. He paused, as if reluctant to go further, to actually give a name to the horror. Then he spoke gravely. "It's basically poliomyelitis. Polio. Only this time the virus is faster and deadlier, and it seems to have appeared out of nowhere."

Polio had once been a widespread killer, attacking more than six hundred fifty thousand people, mostly children. Fatal to about 20 percent of the infected, it receded from the rest like a lethal tide, leaving behind deformed limbs and crippled spines, bodies that would never heal. Dr. Salk's and the Sabin vaccines had eradicated polio, ostensibly for good. There had been only a handful of cases in this country since 1957. But this present, mysterious epidemic had a much higher fatality rate than the polio of old.

It was the second coming of a dreaded disease.

"All of these children were vaccinated?" I asked.

Lavine sighed. "Most of them. It doesn't seem to matter. We're looking at the Son of Polio," he said. "The old menace with a new, more potent kick. It rushed past the standard vaccine without blinking. Some of the World Health people think a broken sewer line contaminated a water source, and that's how it spread. But in Los Angeles we don't know how the hell it originated. Here. Or in Boston. Or wherever it breaks out next. And we certainly don't know how to stop it."

As if to emphasize his point, he looked around at the sick children—the dying children. I shuddered to think how many of them wouldn't be going home.

"They can't stop it in Boston, either," I replied. "They don't know how this could have happened. But it did. What the hell is going on?"

3

Rome, one week earlier.

Father Nicholas Rosetti had never been so focused—and yet so devoid of original and illuminating thought—in his life. He knew all about the terrible "mysteries": the tragedies in Los Angeles, in Boston, and elsewhere. He knew much more, too—so much more that his mind was threatening to implode. He thought he knew *why* the plagues were happening, why the chaos was spreading. *He knew the unthinkable.*

Nicholas Rosetti's workman's build spoke of years of hard labor and outdoor life. He dressed simply but well. His smile was disarming and self-assured, even in moments of crisis and panic. He was darkly handsome, which was inconvenient for a priest.

He'd been born to poor, simple parents, but Nicholas was brilliant and ambitious. He understood how powerful the Church was and, more important, how powerful it could be. He knew, he just *knew,* that one day he would be a cardinal.

But an odd and unexpected thing happened to him when he was ordained a priest: Nicholas Rosetti started to believe. Suddenly given the divine gift of faith, he promised God that he would dedicate his life to serving the Church and its people. That was how he came to the attention of the Holy See, and then Pope Pius himself. Father Rosetti was as smart as any priest in Rome, but he wasn't power-hungry. He was a loyal, genuinely good man, and he actually *believed*.

As he walked he found himself gazing up at the huge, ornate domes of St. Peter's Basilica. He was looking for answers but finding none. His already brisk pace accelerated.

As he struck out across the familiar, teeming St. Peter's Square— that majestic piazza ringed by stone Bernini colonnades—he could still hear the recent words of His Holiness Pope Pius XIII. They rang in his ears, louder than the din of the Roman streets.

Faithful Nicholas, Pope Pius had said, *I want you to investigate a miracle for me. Actually, two miracles. You can tell no one. You will be alone.*

Nicholas Rosetti strode past the four magnificent candelabra built at the base of the Egyptian obelisk that had once towered in the center ring of the Circus of Nero. He still couldn't believe that the pope—the world's most powerful spiritual leader—had chosen *him*.

Eighty-one years ago, a message was given to three children at Fátima, Portugal, by Mary, Our Blessed Lady. As you know, the secret of Fátima has never been revealed. Circumstances dictate that I must now tell you of the extraordinary message. I must tell you this secret, but you can tell no one. . . . It's vitally important, Nicholas. It has to do with the polio outbreak in America, the famines in Asia and Africa, so much more. . . . Everything is connected. You'll see for yourself soon enough.

Rosetti had already come to the Porta Sant'Anna. He was about to leave *Città del Vaticano*, the 109-acre papal state of Vatican

City. *And will I also be leaving its protection?* he wondered. *Am I truly alone now?*

As he turned down the ancient, crumbling Via di Porta Angelica, the priest felt a curious surge of dizziness. Disoriented, he paused, gripped by a kind of swooping vertigo.

He felt that he was being...*watched.*

Shooting pains engulfed his chest, like knives piercing into his heart. His vision dimmed. He saw only a narrow pinprick of light.

"Oh, God," he gasped. "What's happening to me? What's happening?"

Suddenly he heard a voice—deep and powerful. *There is no God, you fool. There never has been. Never! There is no way a human fool could ever know God.*

He tried to steady himself, grabbing on to a lamppost as a tide of nausea swept over him.

"That man is sick," someone shouted in Italian. "Look at him! Someone help!"

Nicholas Rosetti gasped as his throat constricted. Excruciating pain lanced down his left arm and entered his leg. It felt like he was being skewered alive.

He again heard the Voice, deep inside his head. *You are going to die. Know that your life meant nothing.*

Could he be having a heart attack? He was thirty-six and healthy as a horse. He'd jogged five miles along the Tiber that morning.

He fell to the cold stone pavement. The sky seemed to be receding above him, as if being pulled away into space. Colors swam before his eyes. Faces looked down at him, blurred in his sight. They were grotesque, changing form and shape.

He recalled the incredible revelation he'd received just moments before, deep inside the gold-domed Apostolic Palace.

I must tell you the secret, Pius had said. *Listen closely, Father Rosetti. Our Lady of Fátima promised the world a divine child. It's happening now. You must find the virgin mother, Nicholas. Only she can stop the chaos, the plagues around the world. You must find her.*

Nicholas Rosetti lay gasping in the street. "Please, help me," he heaved. "I can't die now. I know the secret."

"We all know it," whispered someone in the crowd gathered over him.

"We all know the secret," they said in chorus. They smiled down at him. *"We all know!"*

And he saw now that they were devils—every one of them. The streets were filled with monstrous, snarling devils.

He heard the Voice again.

You're going to an early grave with your precious secret, Nicholas. You're going straight to the Kingdom of Hell.

4

Newport, Rhode Island.

Kathleen Beavier nervously scratched at the ragged red scar on her wrist. The seventeen-year-old tried not to think about the night she'd cut herself in Boston. Months had passed, but of course she couldn't forget.

She glanced at the *Boston Globe* on the breakfast table beside her. The headline screamed about a mysterious outbreak of polio in Boston. Was the whole world going crazy lately? It seemed like it.

Or maybe it was just her.

She shivered suddenly. She had the sense that there was something wrong with the air in the house. It was suffocating and nasty. It seemed almost evil to her.

Almost *alive*.

Stop it. Just stop it, Kathleen commanded herself.

But she had thoughts like this all the time now. She heard voices. Had crazy ideas. Ever since South Boston, she'd wondered if she might be a little insane. But who wouldn't go kind of nuts under the circumstances?

She turned the newspaper over. No need for bad news right now.

A figure moved across her vision.

"I don't want any breakfast," she said to the housekeeper, Mrs. Walsh.

"Don't talk to me like that, Kathleen," Mrs. W. scolded mildly. The white-haired woman set down a tempting little tray of goodies: fresh fruit, cereal, bread warm from the oven. The breakfast table on the veranda looked out over the rocky shoreline behind the Beavier house in Newport, Rhode Island.

Kathleen reluctantly smiled. Despite her wish to be stubborn and starve herself, to just say no, she stuck her spoon into the muesli.

"Blech," she said.

"You're very, very welcome," said Mrs. Walsh. She'd been the Beaviers' housekeeper since before Kathleen was born, and she had little patience for teen angst.

Kathleen played with the cereal and the mandarin orange sections and the seven-grain toast on her tray. She sipped her coffee and wished, for the millionth time, that it didn't have to be decaf. Then, slowly, heavily, she extricated herself from chair and table. "Thanks, Mrs. W.," she said out of habit.

"Be careful, Kathleen," Mrs. Walsh called after her.

It made her smile. Careful? Really? Wasn't it a little *late* for that?

5

Supporting her protruding stomach with her left hand, Kathleen negotiated the steep flight of bleached wooden stairs down to the sand. Her one guiltless pleasure lately was the beach, and it lay directly ahead.

She could cry on the beach. She could scream all she wanted to, and her voice would be drowned out by the crashing waves. She could act crazy if she wanted to. And she very much wanted to. She was eight months pregnant, and that was just one of the things that made no sense to her. The doctor who was supposed to perform the abortion had either committed suicide or been murdered—the police still didn't know.

Kathleen might have died that night if another patient hadn't arrived and found her bleeding on the floor.

She sighed as she reached the beach. Her swollen feet felt like they were bursting out of her Prada lace-ups. She would have untied them, but she couldn't see them, let alone reach that far down.

How had this happened to her? *How? Why?*

Wading through the ocean's low tide, soaking her shoes and socks, she made the gesture pregnant women everywhere make: She rubbed a soothing circle on the warm, tight skin of her stomach.

She wanted to hate it, but no matter how angry she was, this baby was hers. She couldn't be mad at it. Her baby hadn't done anything wrong.

She stood with her face to the early-morning wind, somewhat mild for early October, and watched a dozen sandpipers scrambling in and out of the frothy surf on tiny matchstick legs.

The gray-and-white birds watched her right back. A swooping gull, too, seemed to stare.

Was it her imagination? Or was this legitimately another one of the weird things she'd experienced since her old life had been taken over by this new one?

She sighed. Gently stroked her belly again. A thought about the polio epidemic jumped into her head. She forced it out.

Stop, she thought to herself. *Enjoy the morning before your parents get up.* The nervous, embarrassed looks everybody gave her made her feel sick.

Kathleen walked away from the water and up toward the dunes. As she brushed her way through the high yellow grass, something darted out and stood directly in her path.

A red squirrel stood on its hind legs, chittering. Its beady black eyes gazed right into hers.

"What's up with you?" she asked it.

As she glanced up toward her elegant, white-frame Victorian home, she noticed a second red squirrel. It was staring at her from a branch of a tree.

And there was a big gray one hunched over, lumbering forward like a tiny bear. *Coming at her? Watching her?*

24

Kathleen heard a screeching cry above her head. Looking up, she saw the flapping white wings of half a dozen circling gulls. Swooping. Kiting. Sailing over the gray beach like rudderless ships.

Were these birds keeping an eye on her, too?

Watching?

Kathleen heard a whirring, the buzzing of insects, in the waving dune grass.

A cloud of blackflies appeared just above the grass.

Watching?

She started to cough; she waved both hands in front of her face.

Down the beach, two usually friendly golden retrievers began to bark.

Other neighborhood dogs took up the howling, yelping, whining, baying.

Kathleen's heartbeat quickened.

The squirrels.

The screeching gulls.

The buzzing insects.

The thick cloud of blackflies.

The howling dogs.

They all seemed to be gathering in a tightening ring around her. They hated her, didn't they? *Am I going crazy?*

"Stop it! Stop it! Stop it!" she screamed. "Just fucking *stop it!*"

Cradling her swollen stomach with both hands, Kathleen hurried back to her house. Her chest heaved with great choking sobs.

She slammed the front door behind her and ran into the parlor. She was breathing heavily as she stood before the huge window and watched the morning sun continue its climb over the ocean.

She hadn't imagined any of it. She knew that she hadn't.

They *were* all watching her.

6

The highway sign up ahead read NEWPORT, R.I. 30 MILES. I'd traveled from Los Angeles back to Boston, and now I was heading toward my third destination in two days.

My windshield wipers cleared a half-moon tunnel over the slick, gray interstate. I felt lost, a little confused, and very tired. I couldn't stop seeing those poor children at Cedars-Sinai Medical Center.

The late-afternoon rainstorm pounded ominously on the roof of my nine-year-old BMW. I kept my concentration on the blurred white lines that sliced the interstate into curving, sliding, equal parts.

I had the speedometer at 75, like I was still running away from the dying kids—even as I sped toward Newport and the very strange assignment I'd recently gotten from the Archdiocese of Boston.

What could the polio epidemics in L.A. and Boston have to do with a young girl in Newport? And why had the Church asked me to investigate? Sure, Cardinal Rooney liked and trusted me. But I wasn't exactly the most seasoned PI they could have found.

I couldn't make sense of it, and that bothered me. I thought back to a conversation that morning with Cardinal Rooney. His voice on the telephone had been as persuasive as ever. "The situation is also being monitored by the Vatican," he'd told me. "They're sending their own investigator. I don't care, Anne. I want you in Newport."

Four years before, when I'd told him why I could no longer be a nun, he'd been sympathetic and accepting. I'd never forgotten that. In a way, I felt like I owed him.

After leaving the convent at nineteen, I went straight to Harvard. I finished at twenty-one, with a thesis ("Firewalking: The Journey from Ages Twelve to Twenty") that became part of an influential book on adolescent psychotherapy.

I didn't have friends; I had work. I'd taken a job with the Boston Police Department as a way of paying my way through school, and I found out that I liked the work. I enjoyed everything except the old-boy network at the top. So right before I graduated from Harvard, I got a license as a private investigator.

My nun's habit was in mothballs, and I'd thought that I'd seen my last of the Archdiocese of Boston.

I was wrong.

The cardinal had kept me in his active file. He sent a note every time I was mentioned in the newspaper. He hired me to work on a few delicate cases. Heck, he sent me Christmas cards, and I didn't think anything of it.

I should have known that Rooney was keeping tabs on me for a reason. And apparently that reason had arrived.

My drive from Boston to Newport had already taken two hours with heavy traffic, and during that time I went over and over everything Rooney had said to me. "There's a seventeen-year-old girl in Newport," he'd confided. "She's a virgin, Anne. And she's pregnant. I need for you to check her out."

I respected the cardinal, but I couldn't contain myself. "It's got to be a hoax," I'd said. "This is the twenty-first century. This is America! I doubt there are any seventeen-year-old virgins *left*."

He laughed and admitted that that had been his first reaction, too. "But you have to listen, Anne," he'd said. "Humor me. You know the younger generation a lot better than I do, because despite all your accomplishments, you're still part of it yourself. If this girl Kathleen Beavier is on the level in any way, you'll know. If it's total bunk, you'll know that, too. Do what you do—*investigate*."

"And let the pieces fall where they will? You have no problem with that, Eminence?"

"Absolutely none. You have free rein on this. Just make sure you don't get hit by any falling pieces."

It was the second time that Rooney had alluded to danger, but an excited chill had come over me. I didn't mind danger. Sometimes I even liked to court it.

I exited the highway and cruised down the pretty streets of Newport. I couldn't wait to meet Kathleen Beavier. I was trying hard not to be biased against her, but I couldn't help it.

The truth was, I just didn't believe in virgin births anymore.

7

I was met at the front door by the Beaviers' housekeeper, who briefly introduced me to Mrs. Beavier and then showed me to my "room at the cottage." Apparently I would be staying the night.

It was only 62 degrees in the room, but I'd worked up a little nervous sweat thinking about this assignment. I'd arrived at the large manor house called Sun Cottage at four thirty; now I stood at a large bay window in a yellow bedroom suite, gazing out over the back of the estate at an unbeatable ocean view. I was lost in thought until a knock at the door roused me. "Yes? Who is it, please?"

A soft mumble came from the hallway. "It's Mrs. Walsh. I've come to draw you a bath, Ms. Fitzgerald. Is that all right?"

"That would be...wonderful," I said, trying to conceal my surprise. "Please, come in."

Mrs. Walsh, a slight woman with a curly, snow-white cap of hair, stood in the doorway. She nodded, then scurried to the adjoining bathroom. I watched through the open door in mild amazement as she sprinkled bath oil under the torrent streaming from the shiny brass taps.

"Your bath is nearly ready," the housekeeper said, ducking her head, then brushing past me quickly—almost as if she were nervous about something.

My bath is nearly ready. Wow. Okay, I can handle this. In fact, I could get used to it.

She was gone before I could thank her.

Entering the bathroom, I drank in the stunning details: the antique brass towel racks, the wood-paneled glass cabinets overflowing with thick bath sheets, the claw-foot tub, and a magnificent pier glass mirror.

I dropped my white blouse and black cigarette pants to the floor and stared at my image in the glass.

I had entered the novitiate at fourteen, before my body matured. I was a novice at the Dominican convent in Boston, where the mirrors built into the walls of St. Mary's were blacked out with paint. For a couple of years, I wore a full habit, complete with wimple and oxford shoes. Even when I was alone, I put on and removed my plain cotton underwear under my voluminous nightgown. My hair was covered day and night. Mortification of the senses, it was called.

Deny the body; praise the Lord. For years I had done just that.

I understood now that I had entered St. Mary's as an escape from my house in Dorchester. I was the youngest of eleven Fitzgerald children. My mother was a cleaning lady and a functioning alcoholic. My father was an insurance salesman but his alcoholism wasn't exactly functional.

Soon after learning about St. Mary's from a sympathetic sister at my grammar school, I joined the convent. I was "the tough one from Dorchester," which served me pretty well. The sisters were good to me; some loved me better than my parents had, and they tried to save me. Who knows, maybe they succeeded.

I would have been shocked to peek into my future. To see my long, shiny hair, my high cheekbones, my grown-up-woman's body. I stared into the steamy pier glass, still awed, amazed, and amused that I'd emerged from my nun-y duckling feathers with what could pass for a model's body. Well, almost.

With a little help from Photoshop.

I smiled to myself and settled into the hot, fragrant bath.

I had one moment of pure hedonistic pleasure before a chill invaded me, and I remembered exactly who and where I was. I wasn't a pampered debutante at the Canyon Ranch spa. I was a hired hand in the Beavier house in Newport, Rhode Island. And I was here to investigate a virgin birth.

Life could not possibly be stranger.

8

A little after five o'clock, I peeked into a large, softly sunlit library, feeling like an intruder in someone else's dream. I heard a woman's voice before I saw anyone. "Good evening, Ms. Fitzgerald."

Carolyn Beavier was standing in front of a wall of floor-to-ceiling windows that looked out over a green lawn rolling all the way down to the ocean. She was in her late forties, with a smooth oval face and prominent cheekbones. Her straight blond hair was held back by a simple velvet band. Everything about her was elegant. Moneyed.

She introduced me to her husband, Charles, a silver-haired man with the sharp, angled look of a corporate warrior. He wore a charcoal-gray business suit, a crisp white shirt with gold cuff links, and a striped silk tie.

He acknowledged me politely, then bent over a handsome writing desk and snapped closed the latches of a black briefcase. Carolyn sank into a sofa covered in ivory linen and invited me to sit in a nearby dove-gray slipper chair.

Charles Beavier said, "You've got impressive credentials, Ms. Fitzgerald. A degree in adolescent psychology from Harvard. Experience with disturbed children at McLean Hospital in Belmont. And numerous published articles about teenagers and the...*unique* challenges they present to their parents. You must be much older than you look."

"No," I said, offering him a small smile. "Just faster."

He raised an eyebrow but said nothing. I didn't feel the need to explain how I'd finished college so quickly, or how I'd pulled more all-nighters writing and researching than I could count. And since Cardinal Rooney hadn't included my experience in police work as part of my background, I decided not to mention that now, either.

"But credentials aside," Charles Beavier said, "I don't see how you can help us."

"We're under so much stress," Carolyn broke in.

"I understand," I said, although I didn't—not yet.

"You really *can't* understand the strain," Charles Beavier said roughly. "When we learned Kathleen was pregnant, I wanted to strangle her—" His voice caught in his throat.

Carolyn finished for him. "It wasn't just the pregnancy. It was that Kathleen hadn't told us. Then, as you know, she tried to kill herself. I wish she'd tried to kill me instead."

"Stop it," Charles Beavier said. "It's not your fault, Cee."

But his wife ignored him. "I wish Kathleen and I were closer. I wish I'd made more time for her. I wish, I wish." Her hands twisted in her lap.

I sensed that Carolyn Beavier wasn't a carpool–field hockey kind of mom. She was more like royalty: a queen of the Newport–Boston–New York social scene. A society woman married to a

33

corporate chieftain, she probably spent more time cultivating her pet charity than she did raising her own daughter. And Charles? He basically lived in boardrooms, on country club golf courses—it was obvious.

"Kathleen and I do love each other," she added softly, "but we're not close enough. Especially now." She stared down at her feet in their patent-leather flats. "We've never really been friends."

"Stop blaming yourself," Charles Beavier interrupted. "You didn't get her pregnant, Cee. You didn't slit her wrists in an abortion clinic in Southie."

He sounded tough—cruel, even. Then, surprisingly, he choked, and two fat tears rolled down his face.

What a scene. I reached out a hand impulsively—and to my surprise he squeezed it. Then he took his hand back from mine and pressed a folded white handkerchief to his eyes.

"Sorry," he said, looking at me again. "We *are* under a lot of stress."

"I hope you can both try to take it easy on yourselves," I said. "I'm not here to judge anyone. I'm here to help Kathleen, if I can. And to represent the archdiocese."

Carolyn Beavier smiled weakly. "I'm certain you'll get along with her. She's sweet and loving. She's a very good girl."

I nodded. "I'm sure she is. Can you...can you try to tell me what happened?"

Charles sat down beside his wife on the sofa and took her hand. "I'll start at the beginning. As much as we know about the beginning," he said in a grave tone.

Stopping and starting as he sorted through the details, Charles Beavier attempted to explain. They had always trusted Kathleen, he said. They'd never been given a reason not to. Then came the news of her pregnancy, which had been a terrible shock. And then, far worse, the near tragedy of her attempted suicide.

34

"It was when we were nursing her back to health that Kathleen told us she was still a virgin," Carolyn said softly.

"A pregnant virgin? Give me a break. How were we supposed to believe that?" Charles Beavier asked. "If she was lying, it was a scandal that would stain her reputation forever. If she was telling the truth, then she was a medical freak—"

"—or the mother of our Savior," Carolyn whispered.

Her words hung in the air as we all seemed to hold our breath.

The silence was broken by another voice that came from behind us, in the doorway to the library.

"I'd like to try and answer Ms. Fitzgerald's questions."

9

A teenage girl stood beside a huge barrister bookcase, its shelves full of leather-bound books with embossed gilt spines.

She was fine-featured and unusually pretty, with long blond hair in cascading waves down her shoulders. She wore black leggings and a cashmere sweater. She had a gold cuff bracelet on her wrist, and her feet were bare. She could have been a picture in a J.Crew catalogue—except for her enormous stomach, the belly of a woman eight months pregnant.

Obviously, this was Kathleen Beavier.

I searched her face for signs of depression, worry, or fear, but there was nothing. She held her head high. Her eyes were bright and clear. She didn't look anything like a troubled kid who'd tried to kill herself a few months back.

"I was told you were coming," she said. "I'm Kathleen." She patted her huge stomach. "And this is...well, I don't know yet." She smiled quite dazzlingly—and bravely, I couldn't help thinking.

"Hello, Kathleen," I said. I tried to stand, but my legs felt suddenly weak. I was clutching the arms of the chair so hard I was sure I was leaving nail marks.

That warm, serene smile: I'd seen it before.

The lovely face of Kathleen Beavier reminded me of the Blessed Virgin Mary, gazing down from the altar onto our messed-up world.

There really was no mistaking it.

10

Maam Cross, Ireland.

A week had passed since the brutal and mysterious attack on Nicholas Rosetti outside the Vatican gates. He looked much older now. And he felt even older.

He also felt that someone was watching him. He thought he knew who it was, and what it wanted. His only defense was his iron will to serve his Church at any cost to himself.

The doctors who had attended to his affliction could offer no explanation. Tests revealed nothing. *Nothing.* Meaning what? That the attack had all been in his mind? He'd been deathly ill for five days. And then, one morning, the shooting pains, high fever, and blackouts had left him as quickly as they had appeared.

So am I all right now?

Am I cured?

Am I sane?

With grave determination, Father Rosetti drove his rental Fiat over the Irish hills and along narrow, twisting roads. He hardly noticed the beauty of the high blue sky or the bright fall wildflowers. He didn't observe the lush green fields that flanked his path, or the old stone walls that ran alongside them like rocky spines.

His 225-kilometer trek from Dublin's O'Connell Street to Maam Cross in Galway was almost over. But he knew his real journey had only just begun.

As he got closer to Maam Cross, his anxiety about another physical attack increased. His hands began to shake. He desperately wanted to control the fear, but he found that he couldn't.

Why did he sense he was being watched? He could see no one else on the roads.

And he hadn't heard the deep, terrifying Voice in a couple of days.

Maybe everything will be okay.

But that seems unlikely.

He asked directions at the gas station on the outskirts of the almost medieval village of Maam Cross. A gruff mechanic in a greasy cap and blackened coveralls directed him farther west.

After another two miles, Father Rosetti saw stone gateposts marking the beginning of a long, curving drive. Elm branches moved overhead, sending shifting shadows across the car's windshield. The parkland on both sides of the driveway looked unnaturally lonely.

He gave a sigh of relief when he saw that the road came to a halt at the forecourt of a handsome and secure-looking stone manse.

The Holy Trinity School for Girls.

Yes, this was the place.

The girl was here. The virgin Colleen.

If he could believe that.

He parked the Fiat and made his way up the broad stone steps. He could hear a class of girls through an open latticed window, the sweetly monotonous chant of Latin conjugation. *Amo, amas, amat . . .*

How simple it would be to recite Latin verbs the way he had when he was a boy! Instead he was faced with a litany of impossible ideas connected to an outrageous prophecy made decades ago in the tiny parish of Fátima, Portugal.

A virgin here in the Republic of Ireland, eight months gone with child.

A sixteen-year-old schoolgirl named Colleen Deirdre Galaher.

A secret that Rome and the church in Ireland were struggling to keep contained.

And *that* was just the start of things.

Father Rosetti lifted the heavy ring knocker on the school's front door. His heart was racing, and he felt weighted down with fear. Was he being watched? Followed?

At least the Voice was silent.

A tall, green-eyed girl appeared at the doorway. The Holy Trinity student wore a puffy white blouse, a gray pleated skirt, and conservative black shoes, and she seemed to be expecting him. She curtsied and then silently led Rosetti upstairs to the office of the Reverend Mother.

Still afraid of another attack, he gripped the wooden banister as if he were an old man. It was constantly on his mind now: being struck down with terrible, crippling pain—and then most likely dying in agony. Ceasing to be.

On the second floor, the school's principal ushered him into her small, dank office. "It isn't often we're receiving visitors...much less from Rome," Sister Katherine Dominica said. Her small, pious smile made Rosetti distrust her.

She was surely conflicted about her student Colleen Galaher, and concerned about the purpose of the visitor from Rome, the city of the pope. But Rosetti knew she would not ask probing questions. As a provincial Irish nun, she knew her place.

"This term, Colleen has been studying her lessons at home," Sister Katherine told Rosetti. "The other students—and especially their parents—haven't been kind to her about this...unusual situation."

"It certainly is unusual," Rosetti said. He forced a smile and then tried to offer words that were more sincere. "I'm originally from a small town, Sister. People can be cruel. I think I understand what's happening here."

"If you do, you'll be the first," Sister Katherine said. "I'll take you to see Colleen." The nun then nodded curtly and said, "She's here today, *at your request*."

"My request. And the Vatican's," he reminded her. He made the sign of the cross and followed her down the hall to the school library.

11

So this was the girl that Pope Pius had wanted him to see.

Nicholas Rosetti's heart lurched wildly the moment he saw the sixteen-year-old. His head ached terribly. His fingers trembled. The shock to him was that a month ago—even two weeks ago—he had been stable, strong.

My God, my God, my God.

The girl standing before him had skin as white as milk, with a light sprinkling of freckles across her nose. The ends of her curling red hair looked ragged, as if they'd been chewed off. She was dressed in an old beige raincoat, clean but too thin for the weather. The hem of a red wool dress hung down beneath it. Under the dress, she wore blue jeans. Boy's wool socks, the elastic long since sprung, drooped over battered school shoes with rips along the toes.

His heart continued to beat wildly.

Is this the one? Dear God in Heaven, she is so young, so small.

The bulging stomach seemed a brutal thing for this poor waif of a girl to bear.

"Please sit down," he said. "Please, Colleen. You don't have to stand because I'm here. I'm just a simple priest."

A sister brought in tea and scones and then vanished. Nicholas Rosetti took a single sip of black tea before beginning the formal interview of the Congregation of Sacred Rites. This was the first test. The first of many, if Colleen was indeed the one.

A sixteen-year-old girl who very innocently ascribes her mysterious condition to the will of God the Father, Nicholas Rosetti would enter in his notes later that night. *She is just a child, though. My prayers are with Colleen Galaher. Her features are luminous, as if lit by a glow from within. She seems without guile, an honest young Irish girl. A tenth grader. Imagine that.*

He studied the girl as they talked; he couldn't take his eyes away from her. And then suddenly, Father Rosetti was struck by a wave of feeling so primitive, so primal, that his mind reeled.

He heard the Voice, but there were no words, just laughter. Hideous, gruesome laughter that rang like hellish bells in the priest's ears.

He braced himself for another physical attack, but this feeling was different, shameful. He gripped the edge of the desk and watched the skin under his fingernails go white.

"Are you all right, Father?" asked Colleen. Her voice was sweet, warm with genuine concern.

"Quite all right," said Father Rosetti. But he wasn't.

The Voice spoke: *She's so young, so perfect, so chaste.*

Father Rosetti was mortified to find himself aroused. He was powerfully tempted by this young pregnant girl. He wanted her more than any woman he had ever seen in his life.

Take her right here. You can have her, Nicholas. You won't be her first, though.

Father Rosetti almost fell in his rush to leave the library. As he ran from the convent school, he was shivering uncontrollably.

He met the young virgin, the Voice taunted, *and he liked what he saw.*

12

Newport.

I stood at the top of the wooden steps leading down to the beach and watched Kathleen Beavier on the sand below.

She was tossing small flat stones into the surf, and I could tell she was athletic by the way she threw the rocks. She was so confident, so alive—it seemed impossible to me that she'd tried to kill herself not long ago.

I draped an old blue cashmere sweater around my shoulders and walked down to the beach.

Kathleen smiled and waved when she saw me. "The water's probably too cold these days," she said.

"Unless you're a rock," I said, nodding at the pile she'd been sending into the waves.

She laughed. "Or a plover."

I glanced at the small, busy brown birds darting in and out of the surf. "Exactly," I said.

Kathleen shifted her weight from foot to foot. She wore a

hoodie, jeans, and a pair of UGGs—a cute mix of sloppy and preppy. "I can show you around," she offered. "Before it gets too dark."

"That'd be great," I said.

As we walked up the hill, she told me the history of the Beavier estate, which had once been a working farm. Antique outbuildings, in various stages of picturesque decline, dotted the grounds. What they called Sun Cottage was a huge, beautiful structure, with four imposing wings added on to an impressive Victorian shell.

"There are twenty-four bedrooms and eight bathrooms!" Kathleen said. "It could practically be a boarding school."

"It's amazing," I said. "It's about twenty times the size of the house I grew up in."

"Yeah, it's not exactly a humble stable in Bethlehem," Kathleen said. She smiled quickly at me then. "I thought someone should just get it out in the open."

I laughed. "Consider it out." I was glad it seemed like we could be open with each other. I said, "You know that I'm a private investigator."

She nodded. "Do you get to carry a gun?"

"Everybody asks me that lately. I have a gun, yes. But it's in my suitcase."

We stood at the end of the manicured lawn and looked down at the frothy hem of the sea. I said, "Maybe we should talk about what I know about you—and what I don't."

She took a deep breath. "If we have to."

"We do have to," I said. "That's what I'm here for. But so far all I know for sure is this: You're pregnant, and you say you're a virgin."

She nodded, and her blue eyes seemed to darken. "Strange but true," she said. "And you know I tried to kill myself."

"All right, yes, and I also know that the Archdiocese of Boston is concerned about your condition. They're trying to keep the story quiet, which is totally understandable. But why did they become involved in the first place?"

Kathleen sighed. "Okay. First of all, though, one minor correction. You said the Church was concerned; I'd say they're terrified. The almighty cardinal came here himself. But he couldn't even look me in the eyes. That's very strange. *I* think it is, anyway."

"Fair enough," I said, trying to imagine what Cardinal Rooney must have been thinking.

"After I tried to end the pregnancy—and then *myself*—my mother finally listened to me. She didn't believe me at first. Why would she? But I'd never lied to her. And I'm not lying to her—or to you—now. I can't explain how this happened to me. But it did." A tiny flicker of a smile passed over her face. "When she finally believed me, she went white and said, 'Holy Mother of God!' And I was like, 'Yeah, maybe I am.'" She shook her head. "I mean, just *wow*."

Kathleen was funny, even in these crazy circumstances; I had to hand it to her. "So she called the local church?"

"Yeah. If it had been up to Dad, he would have sent me to Switzerland to have the baby and then made me put it up for adoption."

Kathleen turned somber. She took a handful of beach rocks out of her pocket and began pitching them into the rosebushes. I couldn't help running diagnostics on her as she talked. She didn't seem like a pathological liar. But was she mentally ill? Say, bipolar? One symptom of manic-depressive tendencies was megalomania or delusions of grandeur. Believing that you might be the mother of God could certainly fit under that category.

Kathleen rubbed at the still-livid scar on her wrist, then wrinkled up her face.

"After my mom took my side, my dad called in some New York City gynecologist to the stars. Then I was cross-examined by theologians at Harvard, of all places. After that, all these different priests began to come to the house. And now you!" She shook her head in disbelief. "But you seem much nicer than the others. They must have made a mistake when they chose you. Or else you're just sneaky."

"I'm very sneaky," I said. "Now I want you to start at the beginning. I've heard the story in bits and pieces. But there's something about a day last February. Eight months ago. You'd gone out with a boy after a school dance. Who was he? What was that all about?"

Kathleen turned away, and a door seemed to slam shut on the newly formed trust between us.

"I'm sorry," she said. She shook her head. "I can't tell you about that. Don't go there. I'll talk about anything else."

She covered her face with her hands, and her shoulders began to shake. I wondered if she was conning me or if she was truly upset. I really couldn't tell.

"I'm so scared," she whispered at last. "I feel alone and afraid. People think I'm either a liar or a saint. I'm neither. I'm just me! I'm still just me!"

She took a step toward me, and I reached out and gathered the badly shaking girl into my arms. I could feel her confusion, her terrible loneliness. I had seen it before, but never quite like this. What had happened to Kathleen Beavier?

13

I was agitated after my talk with Kathleen. I liked her. Period. And I knew this posed problems for my professional objectivity.

I spent the remainder of the evening interviewing the staff of five who worked at the house. I tried to do my job as if it were any other. Everyone I talked to loved Kathleen; none thought she was a liar. They *believed* in her.

Later, scrolling through the day's headlines on my laptop, I read more about the polio outbreak (*Death Tolls Rise on the Eastern Seaboard; Hospitals Strain Under Waves of Sick*). But there was also chilling news about famine in India and an unidentified plague ravaging northern China. What was happening—here, in this house, and around the world? I shut the laptop without looking at the pictures of starving children in Mumbai or dying teenagers in Beijing. I just didn't think I could bear it.

At seven thirty, I checked in with Cardinal Rooney. I told him that I was making progress but that there was nothing earth-shattering to report so far. That was when he dropped *his* little bombshell. He was sending a priest from Boston to stay at the Beavier house.

"Father Justin O'Carroll will arrive tomorrow," the cardinal told me. "You know Justin, I believe."

My stomach lurched.

Yes, I know Justin O'Carroll.

Far too well.

I had a late dinner with the family that night, but I couldn't concentrate on the food *or* the polite small talk. Kathleen had gotten under my skin the second I saw her, and now Justin O'Carroll was coming. God give me strength.

Around ten o'clock, I took a walk alone on the grounds. Even though it had been a long day, my mind was in overdrive, and I knew I would have trouble sleeping if I went up to my room.

This is a hoax. It has to be. Now how do I prove it?

And what will that do to Kathleen?

She had warned me to be careful walking around outside, and I thought that seemed like odd advice. This was a beautiful estate in a fancy neighborhood we were talking about—hardly the mean streets. Everything was quiet, not to mention extremely well lit.

I figured that I could handle any danger I found here.

Or that found me.

14

The night air was surprisingly chilly, and it felt almost brittle to me. I'd hoped that the roar of the waves would soothe me, but instead the sound called up an old melancholy that caught me off guard.

I'd been trying to think of something other than the problem of the pregnant virgin. But I wasn't sure that pondering the matter of Justin O'Carroll was a better idea.

Damn, damn, damn. Why is Rooney sending him?

I remembered everything so clearly, though it had been five years. I was eighteen years old and a devout Dominican nun. I knew that I'd made the right choice in entering the convent. But then, the spring of my second year at St. Mary's, something completely unexpected happened. I met Father Justin O'Carroll, originally from County Cork, Ireland. And, against every rule in the order and every shred of will in my heart, I fell in love with him.

I first saw him when he was a caseworker for Catholic Charities in South Boston and I was working in Cardinal Rooney's office on Commonwealth Avenue. He was wearing a plaid flannel shirt, jeans, and beat-up Timberlands. I didn't even know he was a priest.

He was handsome. There was something vaguely Jake Gyllenhaalish about him, especially with his dark hair. The laywomen at the chancery blushed whenever he walked into the room. He had intense blue eyes, thick curls, and a smile you'd never forget.

I had resisted physical temptation before. I knew where it led: eleven kids, for one thing, and, as a bonus, a lifetime of alcoholism. Even as a nun, I'd been hit on by guys who couldn't tell I was a Dominican sister in my street clothes—but I'd also been propositioned by men who *did* know.

And yet there was something magnetic about Justin.

It wasn't just his looks, though they helped. There was an unmistakable air of strength about him, a seemingly fearless individuality, and an apparent indifference to the rude ways of the world. He really was a man with a higher calling: God, to be sure, but also to the poor and the powerless.

He shared my love of books—we'd had our first argument over whether or not Hemingway was overrated—and music. I'd caught him humming Mozart a dozen times and Radiohead a dozen more.

But he was a *priest;* I was a *nun.* And the two of us simply couldn't be together.

Down on the beach near the Beavier house, I took a seat on a driftwood log and stared out at the dark sea. Pictures were flowing into my mind, filling in spaces I'd forgotten were there.

I remembered how dumb and giddy I'd felt when I was around him, and how dumb and guilty that had made me feel. I'd never experienced anything like it before. Justin and I didn't discuss this for the first year of our acquaintance—I just couldn't bear to bring it up. Then I went to an international conference in Washington, DC, a trip that lasted two weeks.

During my second week, I got a midnight phone call. It was Justin.

"What's wrong? Did something happen?" I asked.

"What's wrong," said a dreamy, faraway voice, "is that you're in Washington, and I'm here in Boston. What's wrong is I'm missing you terribly."

I felt my heart seize up in my chest. This was what I'd wanted to hear—but it also had the potential to ruin everything I'd worked for.

I was tempted to hang up the phone. I probably should have. But then Justin kept talking.

"You have no idea how hard it was for me to make this call. I must've stared at my phone for two hours. I feel like a crazy man. But *I had to call you.*"

What could I say? Could I tell Justin that I'd been missing him, too? That constant thoughts of him had been destroying my concentration all week? All month? All *year?*

No. I could not. I would not.

I sank down on the hotel bed. I said, "I'll be back in Boston soon." My voice was cool—almost hard. It was the exact opposite of what I was feeling. And then I told him that I had to get some sleep, and I hung up on him.

It might have been the hardest thing I'd ever done.

When I got back to Boston, I asked for, and received, a transfer to a Catholic-run charity in Danvers, forty-five minutes away. I had taken vows, and I had made a solemn commitment; I couldn't go back on those now.

Justin seemed to understand my decision. He didn't call me; he didn't even email. Slowly, my thoughts turned back to my work. I reminded myself that I had chosen a life of prayer and service...

Then one afternoon he was waiting for me outside the behavioral health division of the Catholic community center where I worked.

"I had to see you again," he said in the quietest voice. "I'm sorry, Anne. I know you were running away from me. I tried not to follow you. But it didn't work."

Could I admit to him then that I felt the same way? That I'd hoped for this moment every day for six months? "It's good to see you," I said. It was all I could manage.

We went for a long walk through the leafy streets of the town. I tried to talk calmly and logically of duty and our higher calling. Justin barely said a word.

I still can't believe I did it. Can't believe I stood in front of a gorgeous man I wanted to love and gazed into his stormy blue eyes, denying everything I felt. Can't believe that when he put his arms around me, I didn't melt.

"Justin," I whispered, "please don't."

"I love you, Anne," he said, still holding me. It was the only time I'd ever heard those words.

I pulled myself away from him. "I don't want to see you again," I said. "I'm sorry. I'm really so sorry." Then I rushed away. I got into my car and drove home, nearly blind with tears.

Months later, I heard that Justin had been transferred to the Holy See in Rome. Not too long after that, I was at Harvard, no longer a nun.

Funny how things work out.

Or don't.

Now, on a windy, deserted beach in Newport, I knew that I wanted to see Justin again. I wanted to tell him about Kathleen Beavier and how she had affected me. But my desire went much deeper than that. Suddenly, the urge was overwhelming, and I didn't know why.

But then again, maybe I did.

Soon, I was going to be twenty-four years old.

I was still a virgin myself.

The next morning there was a visitor sitting in an armchair in the large Beavier library, a slight, gray-haired man in an expensive suit.

"This is Dr. Neil Shapiro," Carolyn Beavier told me. "He's the head of obstetrics at Mount Sinai Hospital in New York."

I shook his hand. "I guess one New York doctor wasn't enough," I said. I couldn't help feeling sorry for Kathleen.

Dr. Shapiro smiled thinly at me. "Dr. Morison is a practicing Catholic," he said. "He may not have been...appropriately skeptical."

I wondered whose idea this was—the Beaviers'? Or the Church's?

I sat beside Carolyn Beavier on the sofa and accepted a mug of coffee from Mrs. Walsh.

"I understand that Kathleen has been examined previously," Dr. Shapiro said, "but I've been asked to see her anyway. Of course, a home gynecological exam radically limits what I'm going to be able to tell you. I'll be using a portable ultrasound unit, for one thing. And since the Church wouldn't permit amniocentesis—"

"Kathleen's child may be a holy child," Carolyn Beavier said.

I nodded, though it still sounded pretty impossible to me. "Amnio means a point-six-percent chance of miscarriage. It would be acceptable to risk that, don't you think?"

"It's up to the family," Shapiro said smoothly. "So, how is our patient?"

"She's fine," Carolyn Beavier said. Her voice was clipped. "She *will* be fine."

She may love Kathleen, I thought, *but she obviously doesn't know her very well.*

"I doubt she'll be excited for the exam," I said. "And I can't say that I blame her. I'll go check on her."

I climbed the narrow stairs to Kathleen's third-floor room. Kathleen was sitting up in bed, thumbing through an issue of *Us Weekly.* Ellie Goulding streamed from a set of wireless speakers. Kathleen looked up at me, the expression on her face plainly showing that she wanted to be left alone. I understood completely.

"Why should I let him examine me?" she asked. "Do I really need another rando poking around in my private parts? It's a total invasion of privacy."

"I get it, I really do," I said.

"Good," she said. "It's settled then. No stranger's giving me a pelvic exam."

I sat down on the edge of her bed. "However," I said gently, "Dr. Shapiro is a doctor with no ax to grind. He doesn't know you, and he's not a Roman Catholic. The public will find him believable. And that's going to make life easier for you. And your parents. And your child."

Kathleen tossed the magazine to the floor. She took a deep breath, held it, and then let it out in a long whoosh. "Fine," she said. "Tell them it's fine." Her lips were quivering, though. I thought she was going to cry, but she managed to hold back the tears. She was a strong kid.

Kind of like how I used to be.

16

"Safe to come in?" Shapiro asked from the doorway.

"Sure, as long as you don't touch me," Kathleen said, settling herself back onto her bed. It was a joke—except that it wasn't.

Dr. Shapiro apologized for the intrusion, and then he sat in a rocker near the window. His eyes scanned the room, taking in the messy bookshelf, the corner piled high with raggedy old stuffed animals, the posters of Frida Kahlo and Jennifer Lawrence as Katniss Everdeen. Very calmly, almost casually, he asked Kathleen questions about her weight, sleep patterns, digestion, and moods. I was surprised that Kathleen's mom had chosen to remain downstairs during the examination.

As they talked, he took Kathleen's blood pressure and temperature and measured her abdomen from pubis to the top of the downward slope. Then he took what looked like a heavy laptop out of his bag.

"This is a portable ultrasound machine," he said. He set it on her bedside table and then attached the transducer with a thick cord. "We can listen to the baby's heart."

He pressed the instrument to Kathleen's abdomen, which he'd slicked with gel. He moved it around for a moment until the sound came to us loud and clear.

The rapid beating of a tiny heart.

Kathleen was entranced, and so was I.

Wasn't that miracle enough?

"One hundred fifty-two beats per minute," Dr. Shapiro said. "Perfect." He paused. "Now, would you mind removing your underpants, Kathleen?"

It was clear that he wasn't asking her permission now. Kathleen bit her lip but complied. "And scoot down to the end of the bed. Thanks, now bend up your legs."

She leaned back and closed her eyes. Sighed deeply. I felt like reaching out for her hand.

"Kathleen," he said, "you've never had sex with a boy?"

"That's right," she said. Her eyes remained shut. "Never. Not in this lifetime, anyway."

"But you've been on dates?"

"Of course. Who hasn't?"

"And you've been kissed and so on?"

"And *so on?*" Kathleen repeated. "What's that mean?"

Dr. Shapiro hesitated. I sensed him trying to rephrase the question in a tactful way.

"You know that a boy doesn't have to put his penis all the way inside you in order for you to conceive?" he said.

Her eyes flashed open. "No one has ever touched me down there," said Kathleen, emotion choking her throat. "No *penis* has touched me down there."

He nodded. "All right, Kathleen, thank you."

"You're absolutely not welcome."

Shapiro signaled to me to assist him. I thought this was weird, not to mention presumptuous, but I helped anyway. He pulled a stool out from under Kathleen's vanity and then brought it to the end of the bed.

"Hold this for me, will you?" he said. He took a slim flashlight from his jacket pocket and handed it to me.

Obediently, I angled the light so that he could see. He placed his hand on her outer thigh, giving her a reassuring pat. Then he tugged on latex surgical gloves.

"There," he said to me, after a moment. "The hymen ring."

Did I want to see it? Not really, but there it was.

The enclosed membrane was soft pink with a vertical squiggle of an opening at its center. The opening was tiny, too small to admit anything larger than a Tampax slender.

Dr. Shapiro shook his head. "I've never seen this before," he whispered.

He seemed to steady himself before he spoke again. "We're all done, Kathleen. You can put your legs down now and get dressed."

He snapped off his rubber gloves and tossed them into the trash can. "This young lady's hymen is definitely intact," he said to me. He shook his head in disbelief.

I almost felt sorry for Dr. Shapiro. His New York expertise hadn't prepared him for a miracle.

17

Colleen Deirdre Galaher was alone in her small room, bundled in woolen blankets to keep away the chill of the night. Outside the village of Maam Cross, less than a dozen people knew about her condition, and few of them paid it any mind.

The virgin Colleen had already been dismissed as either a fraud or a head case by the conservative Church in Ireland. The Vatican would have liked the same anonymity for Kathleen Beavier, but it was more difficult to hide things in a wired-up American city.

As she did every night, Colleen prayed to God and the Blessed Virgin that her baby would be born healthy.

"Just let the child be all right," she whispered, "that's all I ask. Please let my baby lead a good, healthy life. That's all, Lord."

Colleen softly repeated the prayer, over and over, as the wind whipped across the fields outside, through the trees, and up against her house.

"Dear God, I don't know why that priest came from Rome. I

don't even care. I only pray that my baby will be blessed and born in your grace, and *live* in your holy grace."

It was such a simple prayer, and the Irish girl said it beautifully because it came from her heart.

Over and over and over—until she finally fell asleep.

And outside, someone watched over the house and the girl and the child growing inside the girl.

18

John Cardinal Rooney knew that what he was considering was unusual and dangerous, to say the least. He couldn't help that. Not anymore. He'd had lengthy conversations with Dr. Shapiro and Anne Fitzgerald. Then he'd spoken with Charles and Carolyn Beavier.

Finally, he'd gone to St. Catherine's Hospital and wandered through the wards, which were overflowing with sick and dying children. It was his walk among the afflicted children that finally made up his mind. He saw, and felt, a connection between the polio outbreak... and Kathleen Beavier.

Dying children, a virgin birth, he thought, the ice clinking in his glass. *Dear God, how can this be?*

He worriedly rubbed his chilled hands together. The whiskey wasn't helping at all. Perhaps it was because it was so infernally cold that day in Boston.

All across the city, thin plumes of smoke rose in gray-blue

spirals, vanishing into the high, subtly warring skies. All day the story of a possible virgin birth had been building. He wondered how the rumor had started. Who was the leak?

Finally, late on Sunday evening, he wrote out a terse statement from his office high over Commonwealth Avenue.

> In response to the interest in the pregnancy of
> Kathleen Beavier, there will be a press conference
> on Monday. The conference will be held at Sun
> Cottage, the Beavier home in Newport. Kathleen
> Beavier will be present to answer questions.
>
> Admittance will be by invitation only.
>
> Until Monday, God bless all of you. You remain
> in my prayers.

He sat back, read it over twice, and reconsidered going public. A voice deep inside him said, *Yes, you should.* He wondered if the voice was his own or his God's.

Or someone else's.

19

At 9:39 p.m., twenty-five-year-old *New York Daily News* reporter Les Porter was home in his fourth-floor walk-up in the Village. His girlfriend was making a nice dinner, and he'd promised to help—that is, to not obsessively check Twitter, Google alerts, or any of his other internet addictions. But he could feel in his gut that news was breaking.

When his phone dinged with a text from his source in Rome, Porter forgot everything else: the smell of the roast chicken; Renata's amusing anecdote about her potentially insane coworker; their cat, Jimmy Fallon, arching his back, passing his furry tail right under his nose.

"Git," he said, pushing the cat away. "I'm working."

He immediately pinged Tom McGoey, international news editor in New York. He had a confirmation in Rome; now he needed one from Cardinal Rooney's office. So he called Boston. His contact there was Father Justin O'Carroll. O'Carroll was clever and worldly. For a priest.

"Father O'Carroll, can you give me any other confirmation on the story? Anything? Anyone you can send me to? It's in the best interest of all of us to get this absolutely right."

Porter put the phone on mute and yelled for Renata to turn down the Rihanna she'd just started blasting. "Please," he said, "this is important."

She rolled her eyes at him and then took a big sip of wine.

"All right, Father," Porter said, unmuted. "Yes, I understand your problems completely. I'm going to talk with my editor, and I'll call you back. I know how sensitive this story is. Trust me, the *News* will do an honest and fair job with this."

But Porter didn't call his editor. Not right away. The news was too good to wait.

He had 140 characters and no time to waste.

WTF? Virgin birth in Newport, RI? Live updates here and at nydailynews.com.

Then he leaned back in his chair, satisfied with his tweet. "A divine child. A divine fucking American child," Les Porter muttered to himself. "You heard it here first."

20

Rome, the Vatican.

His Holiness Pope Pius XIII lay in his bed with one leg twisted under him. His skin was a sheet of running sores. He was in agony, and he was terrified.

Of the polio epidemics in America.

Of the famines and floods in Asia and Mexico.

Of the pregnant virgin girls.

Of his own mortal body and what was happening to it.

He could still breathe. He could still swallow. But he couldn't move or speak. He lay contorted and helpless in his own soft bed. He couldn't even press one of the buttons on the buzzer system for help.

And the pope found that, for the first time in his life, he could not pray.

He knew that he would be found in his spartan bedchamber the next morning. The camerlengo would confirm his death in the presence of the master of papal liturgical celebrations and a worried knot of other high-ranking Vatican officials. He wondered, *Will I be standing then in God's holy light? Or will I be kept here, a prisoner of my own mind and body?*

He understood that he was not alone. The Devil was with him this very moment, and he had been for what seemed an eternity, mocking his frailty and hurling a storm of grotesque images against the soft, weak tissue of his brain.

But he was not concerned for himself—only for the void his passing would create. His terror was for the people.

And for the virgins, the *two* young girls who had no idea that their destinies were intertwined.

He stared at the wooden crucifix on the wall opposite his bed and wondered in all humility how he had failed God. How he'd been so easily defeated. He wondered if he would even be forgiven. Or if he was about to go to Hell.

He reached out his mind to the young investigator, Father Nicholas Rosetti. Had he told him of the miracle at Fátima? He was no longer sure. But he knew the story as if he'd been there himself.

October 13, 1917: One hundred ten thousand witnesses from all over Europe and as far away as the United States had collected on the hilltops of Portugal. They had stood in the downpour, waiting for the three small children. His father had been one of them.

Torrents of rain had been mercilessly flooding the desolate sheep pasture since before dawn. Thousands of dark umbrellas shrouded the crowd against the chill, numbing rain. The smells of gamy, charred lamb, chicken, and onions thickened the air.

A miracle was expected.

At that time, people still believed in miracles.

At five past one in the afternoon, the three children who had been told the secret prophecies from Mary herself finally appeared. They were wide-eyed and trembling, protected by a tight procession of severe-looking nuns and priests. Behind them came more priests in dripping soutanes, holding flickering red torches and gold crosses.

The children—Francisco, Jacinta, and their cousin Lucia—suddenly began to point toward the whipping black skies.

This was their sixth and last appearance.

"Put down your umbrellas and she will stop the rain!" ten-year-old Lucia cried out.

The little peasant girl's urgent command passed through the swelling crowd.

"Please, madam, your parasol."

"*Senhor,* your umbrella, please."

At 1:18 p.m., October 13, 1917, the black thunderclouds that had cloaked the sky since dawn suddenly separated.

The sprawling festival of people stared upward with open mouths and widening eyes.

A golden glow fanned out along the edge of the clouds. The sun appeared with blinding brilliance.

"Look! The sun has come out!"

"Our Lady is here!"

Thousands knelt in the thick mud. And as it would soon be reported in the *New York Times* and everywhere else, the afternoon sun began to tremble and spin at a terrifying speed toward the earth.

Brilliant light rained down on the transfixed crowd as they watched it spiral back up to the sky.

"Please pray to Our Lady," begged little Lucia. "She says the world war will end soon! She says the Devil will be stopped this time *as a sign!*"

The horde of men and women surrounding the three children pounded their chests and began to yell. "I see her! She is so beautiful! The Mother of God has come back to Earth here at Fátima!"

His Holiness Pope Pius XIII cherished the story his father had told him so many times. He hadn't been there, but he knew it had happened.

He believed.

The Lady had spoken. The Lady had appeared. *And in her secret revelations to the three children, she had foretold everything that was happening now—all of it!*

Then a violent seizure ripped through the cerebrum of the most revered man in Christendom, canceling all but one regretful thought: He would never know which virgin bore the divine child.

21

I am a priest. I'm here on important Church business.

Father Justin O'Carroll stood in a patch of bright sunshine at the foot of the Beavier driveway and tried to catch his breath. This was going to be a challenge.

I am a priest.

He squinted up at the vast white house. Any minute, he'd be seeing Anne Fitzgerald, and he wasn't sure that he wanted to. It had taken him a long time to get over her. He wasn't in the mood to relive the experience.

Was it fate?

Or was it his own design? He'd recommended her services to the cardinal, who had agreed immediately and sent her here. John Rooney said that Anne was a skeptic—with a touch of the cynic, too—and that that was what was needed in Newport.

But he hadn't thought he'd ever see her again.

He could still recall her anger when he'd shown up at the charity where she worked. She'd been calm at first, but eventually she'd let him have it. *You had no right to come here,* she'd said.

He didn't disagree.

Anne is a trial, he thought to himself. A trial he had earned. He'd been selfish before. This time, he wasn't going to inflict his feelings on her.

"Jesus, God," he muttered suddenly. "There she is."

He watched as the lithe, strikingly attractive young woman strode over the dunes toward the main house. And though years had passed, he had the same thought he'd always had: He still loved this woman.

But now he was sensible enough not to show it.

Anne's sure-footed stride was achingly familiar to him, as was the way her thick black hair whipped around in the breeze. She seemed to be walking in slow motion—there could be no other logical reason why it took an eternity for her to reach him.

He felt his insides shift. No amount of steeling himself against her presence had prepared him for this actual moment.

Finally, they stood facing each other in front of the Beavier house. It occurred to him that the impressive, dramatic locale was appropriate for their meeting.

Anne gazed at him, wordless. He wondered if she was furious with him for having surprised her again. He could have called, he knew. Given her a warning.

"Hello, Anne," Justin managed. He was uncharacteristically tongue-tied. "It looks like I'm part of all this intrigue, too."

At last, she ducked her head and murmured a quiet greeting. "Hello, Justin."

That was all. She apparently didn't have anything else to say.

When she looked up at him, he stared into her brown eyes a little longer than he ought to. She looked more lovely than she ever had. It made his heart physically ache to see her again.

"I'm sorry about just coming like this," he offered, "but you don't say no to the cardinal."

"I know, Justin. I'm here for the same reason."

He stood rooted to the driveway, blood pounding in his forehead, watching her features for some small sign of her feelings. Would she tell him she was glad to see him? Or would she turn and walk away?

When her smile finally came, he felt as if he'd been blessed.

Anne held out her slender hand to him. Formal, yet with the warmth of friendship. "I'm glad to see you, Justin. We've got a great deal to do here. Kathleen Beavier is an amazing young woman. But I *don't* believe she's going to be the mother of God."

22

Les Porter stubbed out his second cigarette of the morning and put the ashtray back on the nightstand. From his wide double bed in the Newport Goat Island Hyatt, Les had a pretty great view of the gently arching Newport Bridge.

"What hath God and the *Daily News* wrought?" he muttered under his breath. There was a traffic jam from hell on the bridge—and he used that term advisedly.

Who were these people rushing to Newport? Believers? Curiosity seekers? Ambulance chasers? All of the above, most likely.

The virgin birth story had broken the internet, for starters. Now the networks were going crazy, and 20th Century Fox and Warner Bros. had tried to nail him down for film rights a split-second after he'd signed on with United Talent Agency. His new agents, Richard and Howie, had licked their collective chops and assured him that the Kathleen Beavier story was going to do huge things for him. He'd already known that. This was front-page material into the indefinite future.

First, speculation before the birth, with all of its ingredients of mystery, controversy, religion, and sex—or the possibility thereof.

And then the spectacle of the birth itself.

Was it a hoax?

Or was it for real?

And then what?

Personally, he thought Kathleen was just another attention-seeking teenager, a poor kid desperate for her own reality show, but from his point of view it didn't matter if the Beavier girl was a virgin or a fraud. He had half a million new Twitter followers hanging on his every word.

He'd broken the story—and while he couldn't own it, he could put his fingerprints all over it. And that's what he meant to do.

Les Porter dressed quickly in cords, a cashmere sweater, and an Irish oilskin jacket. His clothes cost more than the maintenance in his co-op apartment. He'd always had a thing for good clothes. Only now, for the first time, the expense was justified. Cameras were going to be pointed *at him* today.

His rental car was waiting outside the Hyatt, and as he pulled out of the parking lot he found himself doing something he couldn't remember having done for fifteen years.

Les Porter, graduate of Regis High School and Manhattan College, quietly said the Lord's Prayer. It wasn't that he believed in the virgin. It was just that . . . with all of his bravado, he couldn't quite *not* believe.

23

The crowds had started to gather early around the Beavier home. The Newport police were there in numbers, and I spent half an hour out on the barricades talking to them. Most of the cops were *highly* skeptical of the so-called virgin birth. Same as me.

"This is just rich people turning adversity to their advantage," one mustached cop grumbled. It was a funny line, but I thought he was dead serious—and maybe dead right.

As the hour of the press conference approached, reporters and a few family friends were allowed onto the grounds of the estate. I talked to several of the Beaviers' friends and relatives, but no one could shed any more light on the mystery.

I was working hard at this but not getting very far. The people I talked to were strictly divided between devout believers and aggressive skeptics. No one had *facts* to offer—only their various and useless opinions.

I noticed three teenage girls being refused admittance to the grounds and watched as they started to make a big deal of it. I thought they might be friends of Kathleen's, so I hurried over to them.

"Can I help you girls?" I asked across the wooden barricades set up by the Newport police.

"Who are *you?*" one of the girls asked. She had about five rings in her ears and a gold hoop through her eyebrow, but she still looked young and wholesome—like she was trying to be a badass but it hadn't quite worked out yet.

"Who am I? Well, right now, I'm the one on the inside of these barricades. Are you friends of Kathleen's?"

"We used to be. Before *this,*" said the group's designated spokesperson.

"Before her parents cut her off from everybody," said a tall blonde with bright coral lipstick. "Now all we can do is text her."

"We're her best friends," said the third girl.

I thought it was funny that Kathleen had never mentioned them, but of course she was just a regular girl before this mess. She must have been actually popular—something I'd never had to think about in the convent.

"All right," I said. "Come on in. She could probably use your support."

I opened a space for them to slide through, and my new cop friends didn't say a word; they must have figured it was all right with the Beaviers.

"Where is she being *held?*" the pierced one asked, still full of attitude.

I couldn't resist. "Down in the cellar," I said. "We have these new, humane handcuffs..."

All three girls looked horrified, and I had to laugh. "She's not being *held*—she lives here, remember? And since I let you in, maybe you shouldn't look at me like I'm the enemy. My name is Anne, and I'm here to help your friend."

Or else discredit her.

"I'm Sara," said the tall blonde.

"Francesca," said the dark-haired, Rubenesque one.

"Chuck," said the pierced ringleader.

"Nice to meet you three," I said to them. "Let's go see your friend."

24

Kathleen couldn't believe that I'd broken the rules and brought her friends into the house, but her face lit up when she saw them grouped at the bedroom door.

"You really gotta lay off the pumpkin spice lattes, girl," Chuck drawled. "You look *super* bloated."

Kathleen surprised me by bursting into laughter. She patted her stomach. "I know, right? I'm just totally addicted."

And then they were hugging one another, all four of them sprawled on Kathleen's giant bed.

I left the girls alone for a few minutes, but when I heard footsteps coming down the hall, I figured it was time to get them out again. No sense in any of us getting in trouble.

"Thank you, thank you, thank you, Anne," Kathleen said as they waved their good-byes. She wiped her eyes—whether they were tears of laughter or sadness or relief, I had no idea. "I really owe you one."

We passed Mrs. Walsh in the hall, and she gave us a disapproving stare.

I took Sara, Francesca, and Chuck down the back stairs to the pantry. "So why were the three of you banned from the house?" I asked.

"The Beaviers are *incredibly uptight* assholes," Francesca spoke up. "That's why. Carolyn treats Kathleen like a porcelain doll—like she'd break if you looked at her funny. And Mr. Beavier's got, like, country club disease."

"What's that?"

Francesca rolled her eyes. "It means all he cares about are what his uptight rich friends think."

"Okay, duly noted," I said. "But where do you guys come in?"

Sara spoke up. "We, uh—we helped Kathleen with the abortion attempt. We went and checked out the clinic for her. We set it all up."

No wonder the Beaviers wanted nothing to do with them, I thought. "But she went there all by herself. Why did you let her go alone?"

Chuck got angry. Her eyes were dark, tiny beads. "She told us her appointment was the *next* day. We would have gone with her. Are you kidding?"

When we got down to the pantry, I stopped walking and looked at the girls. I could tell they liked me better than the Beaviers, but that wasn't saying much.

"So who *are* you?" Sara asked.

I hesitated, then said, "I'm somebody trying to make some sense out of this."

"Yeah, well, join the crowd. This is beyond all of us. I mean, it just *can't* be happening," Sara said.

I nodded. "So you don't believe Kathleen is a virgin?"

They began to whisper among themselves.

"No, actually, we do," Chuck finally said. "Kathleen never lies. She's basically like the most ethical person ever."

"She wouldn't even cheat in government class," Francesca added. "*Everyone* cheats in government."

"What about the mystery man in all of this?" I asked. "Do you know who he is?" I held my breath.

Francesca blurted, "His name is Jamie Jordan the third, and he *isn't* the fucking father. But he *says* he is. He's a total asshole. There's no way he's the father of the new Jesus."

All three girls agreed.

And now I had a name: James Jordan III.

25

The girls had been in the house. *Those insolent, shameless, awful girls! Blasphemers one and all!* Mrs. Walsh could still smell the blond one's perfume.

They were gone now, thank God, but Mrs. Walsh still thought she heard Kathleen talking to someone. Her phone was charging in the kitchen, so who could it be?

Curious, the housekeeper set the clean white linens on the guest room bed. Then she slipped into the dimly lit hallway and tiptoed toward Kathleen's room.

Ida Walsh was right: on the other side of the door there were voices. But she couldn't make out the words.

Was Kathleen saying her prayers before the news conference? Of course she had to be frightened. Even though she was pregnant, Kathleen was still a child herself.

Ida Walsh took a cautious step closer to the girl's room. She hooked her hand around the doorjamb, and as quietly as possible the sixty-year-old woman levered herself into Kathleen's room.

"Sweet Sacred Heart of Jesus," she gasped. Her hands flew to her mouth. She couldn't believe her eyes.

Ida Walsh fell backward. Her right hand fumbled at her chest, searching vainly for the crucifix that always hung from the chain around her neck.

It was gone! The crucifix wasn't there anymore! How could it be gone? Suddenly she couldn't see! She'd been struck blind.

Nor could she hear! She was deaf!

She opened her mouth and bellowed wordlessly. She collapsed to the carpeted floor, moaning and clutching at her eyes.

Then, in a horrible flash of cognition, she *knew*. She'd done this to herself. She was like Lot's wife, who had looked back at Sodom and was turned into a pillar of salt.

She had defied God.

In the split second before she'd been stricken, she had seen Kathleen Beavier talking to someone. Gesturing with great animation. And then—Kathleen had uttered the most vile curses.

Mrs. Walsh had heard a second voice. It was very deep: a man's voice. And it rang out through the room, calling Kathleen "Whore! Satan's whore!" The Voice told her that she had to confess her harlotry to everyone at the press conference.

Only there was no one else in Kathleen's bedroom. No one Ida Walsh could see.

And in the girl's mirror, the housekeeper was sure that she'd glimpsed rising, licking, gold-and-crimson flames.

The very flames of Hell.

"Mother of God, save me," she whispered, and then she convulsed on the floor.

She'd seen Hell with her own eyes, and she believed with all her heart she'd heard the Devil himself speaking to Kathleen.

26

Wet gray mist and patches of fog washed over Sun Cottage as Kathleen was led down the long flight of wooden back-porch steps. The sky was the color of ash, streaked with long purple slashes. I shivered in my thin wool sweater.

I couldn't help thinking of the strange happenings around the world: outbreaks of sickness, famine, an earthquake last night in New Zealand. Life had begun to feel precarious—as if we were all standing on the edge of a cliff, staring down into darkness. Some said the Apocalypse was close at hand. I couldn't believe that, but it was hard to keep the images of chaos and evil out of my head. What did they have to do with a virgin birth?

I saw Kathleen cover her eyes as hundreds of cameras flashed across the darkening lawn. What an incredible photo opportunity this was.

Her family and church leaders formed a tightly protective wall around her as she approached the bank of microphones. Just behind her was John Cardinal Rooney, tall and imposing in his scarlet clerical robes.

Before her stood a hundred or more news reporters, all of them clamoring for the best angle as TV cameras stared at her with insolent red eyes. The road leading to the house was full of news trucks, their satellite dishes pointed to the sky, where a half dozen news choppers hovered noisily overhead.

And then finally, right up in front, I spotted Justin. He'd been sent here because the cardinal had big plans for him—but was there another reason? Had he and I somehow been brought together on purpose? It was hard not to wonder. While I wanted everything to be logical and clear and sane, life had been making that difficult lately.

Kathleen stared out at the chaotic scene and she, too, shivered. I felt for her.

More cameras flashed like strobe lights. She blinked rapidly and her eyes filled with tears as she unconsciously pulled at her loose tunic top, the only thing she could fit into comfortably these days. I knew what she was thinking, because she'd told me: What did all these important people think of her? Did they care at all how she felt, or was she just the latest sensationalist story? Did they believe her? Or were they waiting to expose her as a freak and a fraud?

The press conference had begun. The world had to be told *something*.

27

Kathleen felt utterly numb. For a few seconds, as she stared out at the sea of reporters, her mind went completely blank.

Then she saw Sara, Francesca, and Chuck, clustered together to her right, and that made her feel a little better.

Or maybe worse. She really wasn't sure of anything anymore.

"Go on, child," Cardinal Rooney whispered. "Everything will be fine."

"I've never spoken to a big group like this before," she finally managed to say. Her voice, booming across the lawn, surprised her with its volume.

She turned to Anne, who gave her a nod and a wink of encouragement. "So," Kathleen continued, "I'm not very good at this. To be honest, I did some practicing in the house before. I was terrible." She smiled at her own obvious discomfort, and the crowd seemed to smile back. Then she took a deep breath.

"Last spring," she went on, "I discovered that I was pregnant, although I was—am—still a virgin. I was scared and confused out of my mind, of course. When I finally worked up the courage to tell my parents, they took me to our family doctor, who confirmed the pregnancy...and the virginity."

The crowd was utterly silent, hanging on her every word. But she couldn't tell if they believed her at all.

"There were more tests—by doctors from Boston and New York and Harvard. There were a lot of suspicious questions by all sorts of priests, and finally the Vatican became involved. Last week, another doctor flew here from New York. He also verified that I haven't had...I haven't *done* anything to be pregnant. I'm eight months now. I'm healthy. The child is very healthy. I see him once a month—on the sonogram. That's all there is to say."

A reporter's voice floated up out of the crowd. "Ms. Beavier, you just said 'That's all there is to say.' With all respect to you, why should we accept that? Many of us think there might be much more to this."

Kathleen hesitated. She *felt* like telling them everything.

And then she heard the Voice: *Yes. Do it. Tell them everything! Tell them!*

"Well, there is something that happened to me back in February," Kathleen whispered. Her breathiness was a rumble amplified by the sound equipment.

"Will you tell us what it is, Kathleen?"

Tell them the truth about your fucking child! Yes, yes, yes—do it now!

"I'm sorry." Kathleen shook her head and her satin-blond hair shimmered. "There are some things that I can't tell you about yet. I'm sorry. For now, you have to accept certain things *on faith*."

Kathleen suddenly choked up as the picture-taking accelerated. She was cold and frightened, and totally alone in front of all these microphones. She wanted to give these people the truth—not her tears. But she wasn't able to do it.

"I really don't want it to be this way," she said. "I'm sorry."

Suddenly, she started. Leaned forward. Squinted.

Something was happening near a dark stand of pine trees that stood like giant sentries behind the mass of reporters.

Kathleen's heart began to pound rapidly. The child moved inside her—violently. A strange heat rushed through her, and she was terribly afraid.

She heard the Voice again—*Tell them! Tell the truth, bitch! Tell them whose child it is!*

Kathleen shook her head, then raised her voice above the crowd, above the *other* voice.

"She's here. She's here now!"

The reporters looked back to where Kathleen was pointing.

"Mary has come."

Kathleen's soft blue eyes glazed over. They became distant and peaceful. Her face was beaming.

Every camera moved in for a close-up of the young girl. They all wanted to capture the innocence and rapture of her expression.

"Can't you all see her?" Kathleen whispered. Tears rolled down her cheeks. She began to tremble, and she looked as if she were about to faint.

"Can't you see her? Oh, please God, why me? Why me alone? She's here now and none of you can see her? She's here, I promise you. Oh, God, she's so beautiful! Can't any of you see?"

28

Human beings have always needed to believe in *something*. These days it seemed like everyone wanted to have faith, but they no longer knew how to go about it. And then Kathleen went and changed that.

Later that night, I sat in the den of the Beavier house with Justin, Cardinal Rooney, the Beaviers, and Kathleen, and we watched the reports come in from all over the world.

The clips, played over and over again, never lost their power: Kathleen's beatific smile, a skeptical crowd brought to its knees. A thunderous, resonant chant seemed to spread spontaneously around the globe: *"A miracle! A miracle!"*

Twitter exploded with a video of an eighty-year-old Italian laborer spinning his wife across the magnificent piazza of St. Peter's in Rome. She looked twenty again in his arms as huge golden bells began to toll.

In Berlin, crowds thronged outside the Kaiser-Wilhelm-

Gedächtniskirche, the famous church and war memorial, while in Barcelona, people sang hymns outside the stunning Sagrada Família church.

At St. Patrick's in New York, Cardinal Dolan celebrated an unscheduled High Mass—and then, by popular demand, another one right after the first. Nearly six thousand New Yorkers crowded into the Gothic cathedral.

Cardinal Dolan knew there was a somber message to be delivered, a message of caution. But the congregation didn't seem to want to hear it.

In Dublin, white-and-yellow papal flags flew from the general post office on O'Connell Street, from all the restaurant and pub roofs, from the portal of the famous Gresham Hotel.

At Notre-Dame in Paris, the south tower's great thirteen-ton bell sent out the holy message to the Left Bank's Sorbonne, the Marché aux Fleurs, and Les Halles. In the square around the Eiffel Tower, the tourists, the people watchers, the lovers, and the street entertainers stood still for a solemn moment. They offered a prayer for the young American girl.

And then at midnight, pure white smoke wafted upward from a small chimney in the papal palace in Rome, to the delight of the throngs waiting in St. Peter's Square below for this very sign. "We have a pope," cried the people in ecstasy as ceremonial cannons exploded across Bernini's magnificent piazza.

High in a top-floor window of the gold-domed Apostolic Palace, a tiny figure in a white silk cassock and skullcap appeared. The Holy Father, the new pope, Clement XVI, extended his cloaked arms out over the people.

People in the crowd began to wave to the distant papal figure. "Papa, Papa," they chorused. "Tell us of the virgin."

29

Ireland.

That evening around dinnertime, two nuns from the school and the parish priest paid a visit to the Irish virgin. When Colleen saw the priest's old Volkswagen coming through the fields, she hurried to hide in the attic.

She saw a musty-smelling pile of old clothes and bedsheets in a corner of the room. It was dark there, even with the overhead lightbulb on.

Colleen burrowed underneath the clothes, making sure she was completely covered up. She could see nothing now.

But she could hear everything.

They were in the house now, opening doors and peering into closets, talking—bickering, maybe—and then calling her name.

"Colleen, Colleen, it's Sister Katherine."

"It's Father Flannery. Are you here, Colleen?"

They made their way upstairs and into the bedroom with her mother.

Ma wouldn't help them find her, even if she could. Her memory was nearly gone and she rarely made sense to anyone anymore. Colleen was virtually alone in the house these days—except for the baby, of course.

She cradled her belly carefully with both hands.

"Hello, sweet baby. Don't be afraid. No one is going to hurt you, baby. No one is going to bother us," she whispered. "It's just the two of us, sweet baby. It's just the two of us, but we'll be good. You'll see, sweet baby. We'll take care of each other. We don't need anyone else."

30

Ireland.

Later that same night, Father Nicholas Rosetti boarded a small commuter plane bound for Shannon Airport. He knew where he had to go now. His mission: to speak to the *second* virgin.

Because she lived in such a small and distant village, the story of Colleen Galaher hadn't spread. Father Rosetti wished the same were true in America. What did it say about the two girls—that one posed for a thousand TV cameras while the other remained anonymous in the Irish countryside?

Around him, other passengers slept peacefully, and he couldn't help envying them.

He tried to relax. He hoped the damnable Voice wouldn't come again.

With his seat reclined, his eyes only half open, Nicholas Rosetti scanned his notes on Colleen Galaher. Though they told him nothing new, he reread them again and again. He was becoming obsessive, he knew that.

Suddenly the plane began to shake.

Father Rosetti sat up, his hands gripping the armrests. He was reminded of the attack he suffered in Rome. *What was happening to him?*

Everyone was awake now. Someone started wailing, and beside Rosetti, a couple began to pray.

And then the turboprop engine seemed to explode.

Rosetti covered his head with his arms. The man next to him clutched at his elbow. "We're going down! We're going to die!" he screamed.

The shrieking in the cabin pierced Rosetti's eardrums. Time became elastic and the plane began to descend with a sickening, unrelenting pull.

This can't be happening. It's too much; it just can't be.

But it *was* happening—the plane was going down! It started spiraling as it fell, and clouds whipped past the window like shreds of gauze. The screaming of the passengers got louder and louder.

"Brace, brace," came the voice of the captain.

Rosetti leaned over and grabbed his ankles as hard as he could. He prayed furiously. *In nomine Patris, et Filii, et Spiritus Sancti...* The faces of his mother, his sister, and his older brother flashed before him. And then he saw the face of the virgin Colleen— strikingly, terrifyingly real, as if she were with him on the doomed plane.

He waited to hear the dreaded Voice, but it never came.

The small aircraft dipped steeply to the right, dropping faster and faster. It tore through the tops of the trees and then hit the ground with a deafening crash. There was another explosion... Rosetti's rib cage smashed down on his knees as the craft cart-wheeled, shattered, and flung pieces of itself across the ground.

For one instant, every particle of sound—both human and mechanical—stopped. It just *ceased.*

Rosetti opened his eyes into the black chaos of the plane. With a sudden ear-splitting rush, flames shot back over his head.

I'm going to be burned to death. All of these people are going to die. We are in Hell.

Breathing hard, he unbuckled his seatbelt with trembling fingers. He fell out of his seat—onto the ceiling of the upside-down wreckage.

Nicholas Rosetti grunted in pain. He found his feet, picked his way over luggage and soft, wet objects, instinctively heading toward the opening that had been the emergency door.

Beyond the wreckage, moonlight streamed across an empty field.

He turned back and peered into the flaming cabin. "Is anyone alive?" he shouted.

There was no answer but the roar of the inferno.

He jumped through the hole of crackling flames and fell onto the damp earth. The fresh, cold air seemed to sear his lungs.

Though he knew that everyone else was dead, he stood and gave one last look toward the plane. At that moment, it exploded in a fireball.

It is Hell, isn't it? A gateway straight to Hell.

He smelled gasoline and charred flesh.

He ran on rubbery legs toward the center of the field. His heart banged against his ribs and sobs ripped from his throat.

When he stopped running, Rosetti wiped his forehead with the back of his arm and watched the fire from fifty yards away.

He had a brief, shameful burst of exhilaration—he alone had survived!

But this feeling was quickly replaced by overwhelming grief.

He fell to his knees to pray for the souls of the dead. He remembered the pontiff's solemn words so recently spoken in Rome: *You will be alone.* They washed over him like a benediction.

He stumbled to his feet. He urged himself to think, to plan. If there was a field, there would be a farmhouse. There would be a town.

His shirt and pants were smoke-blackened but intact. He still had his shoes. He had a single, shallow cut on his hand.

You will be alone.

Nicholas Rosetti straightened his coat and set off toward a hedgerow that marked the edge of a road. The next thoughts came fully formed—as if whispered to him by a ghost.

Something or someone is trying to kill you.

And something or someone else wants you alive.

O f course, there were people who knew about Colleen. The
locals kept it to themselves, though. It was their problem,
their bloody business.

Or, more accurately, it was *Colleen's* problem.

The village boys and girls of Maam Cross had become cruel to
her. They called her "the little whore of Liffey Glade." They had a
theory about where she got her so-called miraculous baby, and they
painted it in fierce red letters on the newly whitewashed walls of the
tea shop in town: *Colleen sucks fairie dicks!*

When she came in to do the shopping, she had to pass that horrible sign, and it made her sick to her stomach.

She jingled her coins in her hand. Her father was dead from
cancer, and her mother had been bedridden for three years now.
They made do on their allotment from state and church. It wasn't
much.

DONAL MACCORMACK, FAMILY GROCER was third in a row of

newly repainted storefronts near the village crossroads. Maam Cross had gussied itself up in the hope of attracting tourists: the signs had been gilded and flowerpots hung from the lampposts. Why anyone would ever want to come here, to this tiny, backward hamlet— well, Colleen couldn't imagine.

She wrapped the thin coat she'd bought four years ago at Dunnes in Galway more tightly around her bulging belly. A chimney pot puffed smoke into the dank fall skies and the skinned body of a lamb hung in the store window.

She shivered and went inside.

The store smelled good—like baking bread—and the heat felt delicious. Carefully adding the costs in her head, Colleen put a half dozen eggs, flour, salted herring, milk, honey, and a hunk of farmer cheese in a basket.

Bridey Doyle at the cash register gave her a long, unkind look as she paid. Embarrassed, Colleen hurried out of the store and stepped directly into the path of Michael Colm Sheedy.

"Oh, bloody excuse me, *missus*." Michael feigned a polite smile and followed it up with a mock bow. "Would you believe it," the sixteen-year-old said, shoving his hands back into the pockets of his hoodie. "It's wee Colleen Galaher toting around her giant belly. Still pregnant with the son of God? Is that Himself down there?" He bent down as if to speak to her baby.

Colleen took a step backward. She saw that they weren't alone. John O'Sullivan, Finton Cleary, Liam McInnie, and Michael's girl, Ginny Anne Drury, were all there, no longer in their school uniforms, leaning against the wall of Grubber's Sweet Shop.

They were waiting for her.

Colleen turned away, but Michael put himself in front of her again and blocked her path. "Please, Michael, my mother is very sick. I have to go now."

"Aye, Colleen. This won't take but a minute, darlin'. We'd just like a bit of group discussion here. What we're wanting to know is, did God take you to the cinema *first,* or did he just fuck ye in the backseat of his car?"

Colleen gasped. "Don't say that, Michael."

But he put his arm around her and he lifted tiny Colleen and her shopping bundles right off the sidewalk, up toward the red sun just sinking over the village roofs.

Tears slipped out of her bright green eyes. "Oh, dear God, no, Michael Sheedy!"

" '*Oh, dear God, no, Michael Sheedy!*' " the boy mimicked in a high-pitched, mocking voice.

As his friends fell into laughter, the head bullyboy passed Colleen to John O'Sullivan.

"Quick reflexes, John-o. Don't drop the ball now, the *godhead.*"

John O'Sullivan, nearly twenty-five stone in weight and only sixteen years of age, nearly did drop Colleen. But then he shuffled her along to Liam McInnie, Michael's chief lieutenant, flatterer, and imitator.

"Please, Liam," Colleen cried out. "Ginny Anne, please! Make them stop! I didn't hurt anyone. I'm pregnant!"

The freckled teenager lifted Colleen up higher. "Pregnant with a little bastard, you mean," he yelled. "Aye, you're a whore, Colleen! Never even gave me the time of day! But then, you were screwin' the Lord on High."

The others howled with laughter, and Colleen cried out in fear.

And at that moment, the most peculiar thing happened.

Out of thin air came a brown-and-yellow thrush, flying at the speed of a bullet. The small bird screeched once and then caromed hard off Liam McInnie's head.

The boy dropped Colleen as his hands flew to his face.

"Bloody fucker!" Liam McInnie screamed in pain as the bird dived again. "Oh, you bloody fucker! My eye! Oh, God! My eye!"

Colleen ran, looking back only once. Liam was clasping his face, and blood coursed down his cheeks.

The bird was nowhere to be seen.

It was an angel, Colleen thought. *Heaven must have sent it to stop those awful boys.*

32

New York City.

Nicholas Rosetti awoke with a start. He'd traveled thousands of miles in the last forty-eight hours and neither his mind nor his body could rest.

He'd been thinking about the incredible secret almost all night. He thought he knew why he was being attacked now, though he didn't expect anyone to believe him.

He rose and looked out the window. He was in a hotel room in midtown Manhattan, a city he'd never visited before and one he'd disliked intensely from the moment he entered it. There was a huge traffic jam down below, and he could hear the whine of a police siren above the soft hum of the air-control unit.

After ordering tea and pastries from room service, he showered, cleansing himself of night sweat, and dressed in black pants and a gray wool turtleneck sweater. Then he unbuckled his black satchel.

The bag held all of his work on the investigation. He took out an old newspaper clipping and smoothed its worn creases. It was dated October 14, 1917, and the headline was as stark and powerful as the event itself: MIRACLE AT FÁTIMA.

The reporter for the *Times* had written these words:

> To the astonished minds and eyes of this eager
> crowd whose attitude goes back to biblical times—
> who, pale with fear, with bared heads, dared to look
> up at the sky—the sun clearly trembled violently.
> The sun made abrupt lateral movements never seen
> before. It did a macabre dance across the sky today
> as the Mother of God reportedly "spoke" to three
> small children.

There had been a terrifying warning at Fátima. Even the *Times* admitted as much.

And the secret had been kept for a century.

The most recent evidence sat at the top of his bulging bag: a nineteen-page deposition on his meeting with Colleen Galaher in Maam Cross.

Next came a packet of two- and three-day-old newspaper clippings. Pieces from the *Guardian* of London, the *Los Angeles Times,* the *Observer,* the *Irish Press,* and others. Tales of viral infections spinning out of control, sudden droughts, and strange, inexplicable deaths.

Rosetti felt his neck stiffen. Tension was returning in waves. He was afraid again. He knew he couldn't hide, not even in New York City.

Pope Pius had told him the secret of Fátima. *No, please!* Rosetti had prayed. *I am not worthy!*

But he knew the prophecy was true. He was a believer, and he believed.

Two virgins, born thousands of miles apart.
One girl would bear the Son of God, the Savior.
The other girl would bear the Son of Satan.

BOOK 2

KATHLEEN
AND COLLEEN

33

New York City.

In the afternoon, Nicholas Rosetti fought bottomless despair as he walked down Eighth Avenue. He pushed against the rush-hour pedestrian traffic, wincing at the frequent touch of strangers. He was a mass of tics and nerves; he jumped at every sound, imagined or real.

He felt as if every day, he discovered new rings of Hell.

He marched onward, mourning the recent death of His Holiness Pope Pius. Millions would grieve for him, but Rosetti felt the loss more than anyone. He'd been charged with a mission that he'd had the audacity to accept.

And now he was truly alone.

He could feel evil and desolation everywhere he walked. These New York people were all damned. He could see it in their eyes.

The *Daily News,* slipped under his door that morning, had caused him worry and grief. On the front page, where it most certainly didn't belong, was a story about Kathleen Beavier.

Such an appalling error for this news to be released. But it was typical of America, wasn't it? The whole country was a circus, and there was no such thing as a secret.

But Kathleen Beavier was only one girl—and the entire rest of the world seemed rife with chaos.

The time is close at hand, Rosetti thought. Too close. He could feel the danger everywhere, and it was real.

Everywhere, there were signs of the Beast's presence.

Six hundred thousand dead from drought in the state of Rajasthan. An unspeakable famine in Jordan. Civil war raging in the Middle East. A drug-resistant form of AIDS showing up in China, Africa, and now Spain and Sicily. The new polio crippling the West Coast and breaking out in New England as well. A hemorrhagic plague appearing in southern France, flowering near the miraculous shrine of Lourdes.

The Enemy had come as foretold.

Lucifer's army was here—fallen angels, legions of them.

It was their time.

34

Newport.

I was acutely, painfully aware of Justin's closeness—his *body*—as we walked along the seaside footpath. It was like there was an electric current between us, simultaneously attracting and repelling.

But I wondered if I was the only one who felt it. Three times in the past two days we'd gone off alone, ostensibly to discuss Kathleen Beavier. Justin was the cardinal's point man, and he took his job very seriously. I couldn't tell if he believed Kathleen's story, but he seemed open to all possibilities.

But what about the possibility of *me?*

I understood that, in the end, there could be no such thing. Justin was a *priest*. But I wasn't a nun anymore, and I could think about him any way that I wanted.

"So you must feel like a member of the Beavier family now," Justin said, interrupting my thoughts.

"Not exactly," I said. "The parents are...what should I say? 'Emotionally unavailable' would be the nice way to put it.

'Self-centered, country club–hopping snobs' would be another way. I guess the truth is probably somewhere in between."

Justin laughed. "You know what Matthew said about the rich."

I very nearly snorted. As if my years of Bible study could be forgotten so easily! "Yes," I said. "It's that thing about the camel."

"It is easier for a camel to go through the eye of a needle than for a rich man to enter into the kingdom of God," Justin said. "Just in case you needed a refresher."

"I didn't," I said. "But thanks."

"I'm here to serve," he said lightly.

As we made our way along Newport's famous Cliff Walk—ocean on one side, Gilded Age mansions on the other—what I kept thinking was: *I want to hold him more than anything in the world.*

But I knew I wouldn't.

Why had we been brought together like this again? *Thrown together* was more like it. Was God some kind of sadist?

I found myself walking faster, and Justin hurried to catch up.

"What's the rush?" he asked.

I didn't answer. What could I say? *I sort of feel like I need to run away from you.* I didn't think that'd go over so well.

"Are you okay?" he asked.

"I'm fine," I said firmly.

He gave me a long look. "You know, Anne," he finally said, "you're a tough one sometimes. You seem so open, so free and easy. And yet you hold yourself off from people."

I stopped in the footpath and faced him. "I don't know what you mean," I said, "but I don't like the sound of it."

"You have a beautiful and very special passion for life. I've watched you in Boston. Here in Newport. You've already become Kathleen's confidante in a short space of time, and that's not an accident. You're so ready to help people, to give them what they want.

But I think you're closed off from yourself. I think you're closed off to what *you* want."

"You haven't seen me in *years*, and you have no right to talk to me like that," I snapped. I turned away from him and began jogging up the path. I definitely needed to get away from him now.

I *did* know what I wanted. I just couldn't have it.

35

Kathleen was going insane, just sitting around her house. She felt hemmed in by the walls and trapped by the bulk of her own flesh.

It was still hard to deal with the changes in her body. Her boobs were bigger than her mother's now, and her face was puffy with retained water. She couldn't wear any of her cute clothes anymore, and worst of all, she had *cankles*.

When this was over, would the old Kathleen reappear? Or had that girl vanished forever?

Until the baby came, the only pleasure she had was the beach. Thank God for the beach—though at this point, she had to sneak down to it, because her mother basically wanted her under house arrest. *What if there are paparazzi on the beach?* she'd asked, horrified.

Then I guess they'll take my picture, Kathleen had answered.

But Carolyn Beavier could not be convinced.

Kathleen wrapped a scarf around her neck and crept down the back stairs. She got to the pantry without being heard, which was good, because she didn't want to have to face Mrs. Walsh right now, either. For the past few weeks, her old friend seemed to disapprove of everything that she did or said.

Beyond the pantry, the mudroom was deserted. Kathleen slipped into a pair of TOMS and grabbed her father's yellow cardigan from a hook, buttoning it over her ugly maternity shirt.

Minutes later she was at the shoreline, staring into the hypnotic waves. The sun sparkled on the water, and the wind was calm. It almost felt like summer again. Kathleen took off the sweater and slung it over one arm.

Then a crazy idea occurred to her.

Or maybe it wasn't so crazy at all: she'd read that being in water was good for pregnant women. It gave their bodies a break from all the extra weight they were carrying.

She kicked off her shoes, then quickly removed everything but her bra and her underpants. Before anyone spotted her, she walked right into the ocean.

The water was cool on the surface and downright cold beneath, and it felt unbelievably good swirling around her swollen legs. She squished sand between her toes and almost laughed—she felt like a little kid again.

Kathleen waded in farther. She felt her body and her mind grow lighter. It was almost like being in a trance. Did she dare keep going? Yes, she did. She walked out still more, then took a breath and bent her knees so that the water came up almost to her chin. It felt wonderful.

"Oh, this is heaven," she sighed.

The waves lifted her a little and then put her down. Here was

113

the weightlessness she craved. She wasn't a lumbering elephant anymore—she was a mermaid. She hadn't been this comfortable—this *at peace*—in months.

The next wave had a long, sweet pull, and it drew her away from the beach. She went with the gentle flow. She put her arms out and her head back and floated. The sky's changing colors fascinated her. Blue to pink to purple to indigo...

Kathleen lost track of time. How long had she been out here? With effort, she pulled her head up and began treading water as she got a fix on her position. She was out much farther than she'd thought. How had she floated this far from safety?

Frightened now, she began to stroke, swimming toward land.

It seemed that every yard she advanced was taken away by the outward pull of the tide.

Don't panic, she told herself.

Just keep your eyes on the house and swim.

She wondered how she could have been so stupid. She knew about tides, had known about them her whole life! Something very strange had happened—as if she'd fallen asleep while floating or something. *Was she losing her mind?*

Her arms were aching. She had a stitch in both sides and the cold was sucking the strength from her body. She wanted to call out for help, but there was no one to hear. As if the ocean were a powerful beast with its arms around her waist, Kathleen was pulled down, then dragged under, beneath the waves.

All around her was watery darkness.

Don't be afraid, she heard. It was the Voice, but it was almost soothing.

No! She gulped seawater but managed to find the surface again. Choking, she screamed a long, wordless scream.

Just go with the sea, Kathleen. The sea is the universe and it is eternal. Be the sea!

She pawed at the air futilely, as splintered images flickered before her. Her friends, her mom, her dad, her baby—

The next wave dragged her under again. A sharp pain in her lungs flared, then grew steadily more unbearable before it was quenched by the sea.

She was drowning, and so was her baby.

36

I stopped running when my shoes hit the pavement out on lovely, tree-tented Bellevue Avenue.

What's wrong with me?

I wiped the ridiculous tears from my cheeks with the sleeve of my sweater, then stood beside the towering gates of an ivory-white mansion while I caught my breath.

It was so obvious to me why I'd run away from Justin: I was still in love with him. Was it really so impossible for him to see that?

I was mad at him, too. I wasn't cut off from what I wanted. *He* was. He's the one who was an altar boy from the moment he could walk. And now he was an effing *priest*. He acted so smart and worldly, but how much had he really experienced?

But I couldn't keep obsessing about him. I had to get back to the Beaviers' and make nice with Kathleen's parents. I turned away from the mansion's imposing gates and headed down a narrow walkway to the sand.

Maybe I'd end up spending my life alone. But at least I had the possibility of getting married, having kids—unlike Justin, who'd taken a vow of celibacy.

Which one of us was braver: him, who'd stayed? Or me, who'd left?

I wandered the beach, spinning on this emotional hamster wheel until twilight streaked the sky. As darkness fell, I cast my eyes around to get my bearings. Something on the beach caught my attention.

A lumpy form lying motionless on the sand.

A seal?

No, a person.

A girl with long, golden hair.

37

I charged forward, calling out, *"Kathleen!"*
    I threw myself onto the sand beside her, saying her name over and over. I rolled her onto her back as I felt for a pulse. It was faint and slow, but it was *there*. Her eyes were closed and her breath was shallow. What had happened? Had she gone swimming? Had she done this to herself on purpose... again?

"My God, Kathleen! Open your eyes, honey. Can you hear me?"

She lay there like a stone. She was too heavy to carry, and we were alone on the darkening beach. I grabbed at my pocket for my phone before I realized I'd left it in the house. Cursing, I called her name again. Tried to think in straight lines. I considered my options. There were two.

Stay with her.

Run as fast as I could for help.

"Okay, Kathleen. Kathleen... it's okay."

I reached out and touched her cheek. Her skin was very cool.

Had she taken pills before she went in the water? It was never far from my mind that she'd attempted suicide once before.

Then Kathleen turned her head. She moaned, and her right leg spasmed.

I swear my heart was pounding so hard it nearly exploded.

I saw the streaks of blood along her thighs.

"No," I cried. "Kathleen, please—" As if she could stop the terrible thing from happening.

I heard a shout, and when I turned, I saw Justin running full speed toward us.

"Hurry," I screamed. "Kathleen's losing the child!"

38

When we pulled up in front of the ER, the ambulance's sirens wailing, a half dozen doctors and nurses rushed out to meet us. They whisked Kathleen away on a stretcher and I had to run to keep up.

Now, an hour later, she was conscious. She was pale but calm.

She was the only person I could say that about. The Beaviers were beside themselves, and the doctors agreed that the baby was in trouble. They wanted her to deliver the baby by C-section before it was too late.

Kathleen absolutely refused. "The baby will be fine," she said. "Please, leave us both alone. I just want to rest."

Dr. Armstrong, Kathleen's physician since she was a baby, begged her to let the on-call surgeon intercede. Her parents pleaded with her, too. If the baby was born now, it would survive. If she waited, it might not.

But they couldn't force her, and she knew that.

"Anne—tell them," she begged. "I've seen Mary. She told me not to be afraid."

I took Kathleen's hand. It was still cold. "These people are experts," I said. "Their job is to take care of you."

I thought a cesarean was the right thing to do, too, but something stopped me from saying so. Stopped me from pointing out that, last I heard, the Virgin Mary wasn't in the habit of giving out medical advice.

Kathleen gazed steadily at me without saying anything at all.

I squeezed her cool fingers. "Of course, it's your choice," I said. And then, it was as if I could hear Justin's voice in my ear. *If the baby is born by C-section, the delivery will not be wonderful and special. The birth will bypass the birth canal, and the Church will never claim the child is a miracle.*

Still Kathleen said nothing, her clear blue eyes as serene as still, tiny pools.

"I want you to listen to everyone—to give the doctors their due—and then do what you believe is best." That was all I could say.

She nodded and closed her eyes. Closed us all out.

It was a terrible night. I lost track of the hours I paced the halls in my damp, sandy clothes.

Finally exhausted, I slumped in a chair. I was starting to doze off when I became aware of someone gently shaking me. I opened my eyes to a sobbing Carolyn Beavier. She threw her arms around me.

"She's fine, Kathleen's fine," she said. "The bleeding has stopped and there's no sign of any damage to the baby. It's truly a miracle!"

Later, the young ob-gyn named Dr. Suzuki told me that, no, it wasn't a *miracle,* but it was extraordinary enough to surprise her—as well as the rest of the medical staff at Newport Hospital. The only person who wasn't amazed was Kathleen herself.

"Thanks for trusting me," Kathleen said when I visited her near dawn. "You were the only one who did. You're special, Anne. That's why you're here. You and Father Justin. You're my protectors."

I was glad I'd kept my mouth shut earlier.

I sank down onto the hard vinyl chair in the corner of her room, and I stayed there until Justin peeked in around 7:00 a.m. He gestured for me to come out into the hall. Kathleen was sleeping, so I did.

When I got into the hallway, I saw that Justin was visibly shaken. "What's the matter?" I said, alarmed. "Are you okay?" I started to reach for him, but then I dropped my hand down to my side. It wouldn't help *either* of us to touch.

"Something terrible, Anne," he said in a hushed whisper. "There's been a case of polio. It's as if it followed Kathleen here."

39

Ireland.

Colleen Galaher thought that if she had to stay in her claustro-phobic little cottage any longer, she would finally, once and for all, lose her mind. So, after making sure her ma was comfortable and warm in bed, she sneaked out and went to the stable.

She knew she wasn't supposed to ride a horse, not this far along in her pregnancy, but Grey Lady was a docile old thing. So Colleen saddled her up, mounted her—with difficulty—and rode down the hill on horseback, her hand wrapped in the old mare's mane. She'd been riding this horse almost since the day she could walk. Thinking this, she felt a terrible sadness. She wanted to be a kid again. She wanted her old life back.

She paused to wave at the Travellers in the lower field. Her mother called them tinkers, or gypsies, and told Colleen to stay away from them.

But six months ago, Colleen had been passing the field on her way to her favorite place, Liffey Glade, when a woman with flaming red hair, a purple velvet skirt, and a man's old tweed jacket had beckoned to her.

Not knowing what to do, Colleen had stayed where she was, and so the Traveller had come toward her, crossing herself and whispering prayers, clutching her rosary as if it were a lifeline attached to Heaven itself.

"Come with me, child," the woman had said, her accent seeming to thicken her words.

And Colleen, much to her surprise, found herself dismounting Grey Lady. Moments later, she was accepting a mug of tea inside the woman's old camper van. The woman's name was Margot, and her camper was a marvel of organization. Neat, hand-built shelves held tools, canned goods, and pretty tin boxes. Her bright clothing was arranged according to color, and houseplants flourished on a ledge below the window.

Beside the battery-operated TV was a shrine to the Holy Virgin. There was a beautiful porcelain Madonna, her hand raised in blessing. Dried flowers lay at her feet.

"You've seen her in the flesh as well as the spirit," said Margot. "I know you have. Isn't it true?"

Colleen had turned to her, dumbfounded. What did this strange woman know?

"You love children, Colleen," Margot then said, her voice humble and reverent. And she'd looked pointedly at Colleen's stomach, which had just barely begun to swell.

"I know your secret, little girl. You are just like her. Your secret will change the world."

After leaving Margot, Colleen had taken a long, slow ride toward the north side of town. The large hospital for the county was there; she thought she should visit before it was her time.

So she had tied Grey Lady to an old oak in a field not far from the hospital. Then she walked across the back lawns and entered the small lobby of St. Brendan's.

She felt grown-up and maybe a little brazen as she made her way up the winding staircase to the second-floor maternity ward. She pushed open the swinging doors and was immediately met by a nurse. "May I help you?" she asked.

Just then a woman moaned loudly inside one of the rooms. A moment later, she began to scream.

Almost immediately, and seemingly in sympathy, a second woman down the hall let out a piercing yell.

Colleen leaned against the wall and tried to compose herself. *My God, it sounds so awful. Will I be able to do this when the time comes?*

She listened to the two women as the nurse gazed calmly at her, waiting for Colleen to answer the question.

One of them called out for her husband—then, almost in the same breath, she cursed him.

I'll be alone, Colleen thought. *I have to be so brave.*

She had thought the pre visit to the hospital would be a good idea, but she had been very, very wrong. She was far more anxious now than she'd been before.

"Miss?" the nurse said. And then "Oh, look at the wee thing!"

Colleen turned and saw what had captured the nurse's attention: a new mother carrying her tightly swaddled baby to the nursery. The woman had put her pinkie in the baby's mouth, and the baby, eyes still closed, was noisily sucking on it.

Colleen smiled for what felt the first time in months, and she knew she would be all right. She wasn't going to be alone anymore. She would have her own sweet baby.

40

That was six months ago, and as Colleen passed the Travellers' camp again, she felt uneasy from the memory. She urged Grey Lady on toward the grotto-like clearing that had been a natural shrine long before Christianity, and even before the Druids. It was to serene Liffey Glade that Colleen came when she wanted to be alone.

A clear, briskly flowing stream bubbled through the meadow on its way to Lough Corrib. Pine and spruce trees bent over the water like the arches of a leafy cathedral.

Nearly nine months earlier, in this same spot, something inexplicable had happened to Colleen. Before that night, she'd been known around Maam Cross as a quiet and well-mannered scholarship student at Holy Trinity.

Maybe she'd never been fully accepted by her schoolmates, but she was appreciated by the sisters at the convent school, who saw their younger selves in the shy, intelligent girl. Colleen had felt a kinship with the nuns as well, and she'd recently decided to enter the convent herself.

Then, in a moment in Liffey Glade that now felt as fraught and otherworldly as a fever dream, everything changed. Colleen Galaher became God's—not just in spirit but in body as well.

Today, though, nothing mystical occurred. Today Colleen rode Grey Lady across the sodden grass before dismounting and pushing her way through wet, rustling branches. Then she knelt on the soft carpet of pine needles in the chapel of trees.

Colleen lowered her head of gleaming dark-red hair.

"Dear Father in Heaven, I am your humblest servant. I know you can feel my sadness, and my love for you. Father, I am so lonely now. I am so terribly lonely these nine months."

But deep inside, Colleen Galaher knew that she was not alone.

She wasn't sure who—or what—it was, exactly...

Always, she was being watched.

41

Newport.

I felt like I was creeping closer to believing that Kathleen Beavier's baby was...*special* in some way—and that troubled me more than I could admit. Was my objectivity failing me? Or did I really believe that Kathleen was telling the truth? I'd gone from "This is a fraud" to "There just might be something here."

This afternoon, I had a few hours to myself for almost the first time since arriving at Sun Cottage. Kathleen was resting in the sunroom, and Carolyn and Charles Beavier had gone to town to shop. Mrs. Walsh was baking furiously in the kitchen. And I knew—without meaning to, without trying to pay attention at all—that Justin was taking a run.

I'd looked forward to an investigation of the Beavier library. It was bigger than some municipal libraries I'd been to, a place where I could do actual research. There were shelves upon shelves of history books (everything an ex-nun could want to know about everything from ancient Rome to American manifest destiny), political biographies, and science tomes, not to mention yards of texts on sailing, seashells, gardening, birds, and finance.

By the fireplace, I spotted a section of books on religion. Many of these were so recently purchased that the sales slips were still tucked between the pages.

A fire crackled invitingly. I poured myself a cup of tea and placed a stack of books about the Virgin Mary on a mahogany end table beside a cozy wing chair. This would be a review for me: I'd already read pretty much everything ever written about Mary. I ran my fingertips down the spines of *Our Lady in the Gospels, Our Lady of Fátima,* and *Woman's Mysteries: Ancient and Modern,* before cracking open a book written in the late seventies called *Alone of All Her Sex.*

"The Virgin, sublime model of chastity," the author wrote, "remained for me the most holy being I could ever contemplate, and so potent was her spell that for some years I could not enter a church without pain at all the safety and beauty of the salvation I had forsaken I remember visiting Notre-Dame in Paris and standing in the nave, tears starting in my eyes."

This was the way faith worked, the way it had felt to me. It was the power of Mary that so many women understood.

I thumbed through the books, looking for clues to the situation in Newport. Ironically, there was little in the Bible about Mary. In a way, she was the least known, and by far the most mysterious, of all major biblical figures. And why?

I didn't have to think hard about the answer. Mary was a woman, a mother. The Scripture writers were men.

A lot of things had changed since the birth of Christ, though. This modern blessed event surrounding Kathleen Beavier, *if it was that,* would be the most completely documented birth in almost two thousand years. There would undoubtedly be books and films.

And—I hoped it wasn't too vain of me to hope—I would be standing at the foot of the birthing bed.

Maybe then I would know the whole truth about the virgin Kathleen.

42

I grabbed my peacoat from the hall closet and walked quickly out-side to my car. Within minutes I was sweeping past Newport's famous Bellevue Avenue, heading east to Sachuest Point. That was where Kathleen had apparently gone with a boy after a school dance nearly nine months before. The mysterious and perhaps mystical evening of February 23.

Now that I was away from Sun Cottage, doubt rose up in me again, and I was more confused about Kathleen than ever. When it came down to it, nothing made sense; everything required some faith on my part.

But what if faith and I were kind of on the rocks lately?

Cardinal Rooney apparently believed in Kathleen Beavier, and he was a tough-minded priest of the old school. Justin, too, seemed to believe that a holy child was about to be born.

What made them so sure about her? What did they know? And what was I here in Newport to find out?

These were the facts: Kathleen was a virgin and she was pregnant.

Not so factual: Kathleen had said that she'd seen the Blessed Virgin. I believed *she* believed that. But I couldn't forget that Kathleen had tried to kill herself and had failed. If she thought she was pregnant with the Holy Child, why had she tried to take her life and that of the baby?

Or should I be looking at the other side of that coin? Maybe the question was how she'd been saved that night. The clinic was supposed to be closed for the night, but another patient arriving late had found the dead doctor and the nearly dead Kathleen.

Was that some kind of divine intervention?

Not that God had done a lot of meddling in human affairs recently.

There was also historical perspective to consider. Christianity was based on a belief in miracles: the loaves and fishes, the wondrous healings, the water into wine. Christians all over the world believed in the Virgin Birth, and that Jesus Christ, the Son of God, had walked the earth as a man. Was it truth or was it myth?

I wanted a *fact*. I was starving for just one tiny little fact to prove what I was starting to believe.

As I continued down Memorial Boulevard toward the point, I saw a gold-and-blue sign pointing down a narrow street: LINCOLN HIGH SCHOOL.

I hit the turn signal. There was someone at the school who might give me what I wanted: a little light on this fantastic puzzle. Kathleen's date on the night of February 23.

James Jordan.

Chalk him up as another cold, hard *fact*.

43

I checked my watch as I pointed the car down the tunnel of maple trees whose red leaves were starting to brown and fall. It was 2.57. I was just in time for the end of the school day.

A bell rang out, and instantly a mob of students stampeded out of the school's glass front doors. I had no idea how I'd find my target, but I scanned the crowd anyway. Maybe luck—or fate, or faith—would help me out. The kids poured past me, faces already buried in their phones, thumbs madly tapping.

I was just about to give up when I saw a tall, muscular boy with a bright shock of blond hair falling across his eyes.

He was swaggering, shoving, laughing, everything from his artfully faded jeans to his expensive haircut conveying confidence and privilege.

I'd only seen a tiny picture on Kathleen's Facebook page, but I knew it was him.

James Jordan was big. I figured he was probably six two and

close to two hundred pounds—more man than boy. He was good-looking, but I wouldn't have pegged him as Kathleen's type.

I felt an inkling of...not fear, exactly, but nerves. I'd been cat-called by guys like him a thousand times—when I was a teenager, and when I was a nun, too. I never liked their predatory gaze.

But since he was the one I'd come for, I walked right up to him. And I said, "Hi, are you James Jordan?"

He stopped, turned, and gave me a slow, cool, appraising look.

"I guess that means that you are," I said, forcing a smile I didn't feel. "My name is Anne Fitzgerald. I'm a friend of Kathleen's."

He shot a look at his buddies, all of whom were checking me out and trying to be as crude and obvious about it as possible.

I felt sorry for their mothers.

"Yeah, I'm Jamie. You're a friend of Kathleen's? What kind of friend?"

"I'd like to talk with you for just a few minutes."

I looked him directly in the eye, and I didn't move a muscle. I didn't show any doubt that he would talk to me.

His curiosity won out over the don't-give-a-shit posturing, as I knew it would. It's what I do for a living.

44

His friends were shifting their feet, pawing the ground like a herd of adolescent bulls. They stood too close to me, looked too hard at my face, my body.

"Who are you? You some intern from the *Boston Herald* or something?" a redheaded jock asked.

I knew I didn't look much older than them, but I was worlds smarter. "Who are you?" I countered. "Some freshman?"

His buddies snorted. "Dude, total burn," one of them said, elbowing the redhead. "She thinks you're JV."

I turned back to Jamie. "I'm not a reporter. I'm just a friend."

"Okay," Jamie said after a few long seconds. "Let's walk and talk, friend."

"Oh, really, you're too kind," I said lightly. And then—I was good cop now—I flashed him a dazzling smile.

Jordan smiled back. He decided to like me, right then and there.

And he was enough of an arrogant kid to think that I'd like him, too. He obviously thought he had a gift with the ladies.

There was a side street at the end of the block, lined with pretty little houses, and we turned down it, walking slowly. Jordan was a head taller than me and as thick-chested as a lumberjack. Nothing had ever unsettled this boy. Or at least that's what he wanted the world to believe.

"Okay," he said as we rounded the corner. "You have my attention. Who the hell are you? Really? And what do you want? You aren't Kathleen's friend. That much I know."

"Actually, Jamie, you don't know shit." I told him who I was, but I said very little about my actual assignment. I also gave off major don't-mess-with-me attitude.

"This past February," I said, "you went out with Kathleen Beavier. That's an established fact. The two of you dated at least once."

He shook his head. "I knew this shit was coming. You guys are so predictable. You're another one writing a book, right? So write this, why don't you: I went out with Kathleen Beavier *once*. One date. Plus a few trips to get a Big Mac or something after school."

"How come there was only one date?"

"How come only one date? Well, we can't spread the boy around too thin, can we?" Jordan said.

This kid was too much. Rich, good-looking, and cocky as hell. Would the world ever kick him in the nuts and give him what he deserved? I sure hoped so.

But Jamie's personality wasn't my business—aside from the fact that I couldn't see Kathleen tolerating him for more than half an hour. Sure, they would have made a beautiful couple: total prom king and queen material. But she didn't like cocky people any more than I did.

"Could you be straight with me for one minute? Back on February twenty-third, you took Kathleen to a formal at her school. Then *something* happened. She told me that much. So what was it? What happened?"

Anger flashed across his face. I saw what he would look like as a grown man, and I didn't like it.

"Listen," he said. "Isn't it obvious as the nose on your pretty face? She won't tell because we fucked after the dance. Everybody knows that Kathleen put on a front like she was an ice queen, but trust me, that night she wasn't exactly the frigging Virgin Mary!"

I didn't like the way he was leaning close to me. I didn't like anything about this kid. But I couldn't walk away yet.

"A doctor from New York came here, a *medical expert* with no reason to lie, and I was standing right there when he examined her. Kathleen is *still* a virgin. She never"—I couldn't bring myself to say the word—"did it with anyone. Not you, and not anybody else."

"Bullshit!" he screamed at me. "You're both lying bitches. I fucked her and she knows it!"

Oh, how I hated this kid. And *maybe* I was just about to make a derogatory comment—*then your dick must be the size of a straw, friend*—which would have been incredibly unprofessional. But before I could say a word, he shoved me.

I went down on the ground, hard. I lay on the sidewalk, shocked. My palms hurt where I'd caught myself. I took a deep breath and stared up at that overgrown boy looming above me. And then before he had time to react, I was on my feet and shoving him back.

"You're a real tough guy, right? How tough are you?" I yelled at him. "You gonna hit me for real now?" I kept coming at him. "Answer my questions! What happened that night at Sachuest

Point? Something happened. I can see it in your coward's eyes. I can see right through you."

Suddenly, he turned away—and started loping up the street. I wanted to chase after him, but I knew it wouldn't do any good.

He was lying to me—I was sure of it.

But if Jamie was lying, then Kathleen was not.

45

All I wanted was the simple truth. But isn't that what we were all searching for?

That night I sat in an antique pine rocker beside Kathleen's pretty canopied bed. The moon hung above the ocean like a big yellow balloon, but tonight its beauty failed to move me.

I was still buzzing from my short but very unpleasant interview with Jamie Jordan, and I felt mistrustful of just about everything. I needed to know what terrible thing had happened between Jordan and Kathleen at Sachuest Point.

Kathleen was weak and exhausted; I could see it on her face. The darkened bedroom was lit only by a small lamp on the nightstand. I turned on her iPod, and Adele's latest ballad of heartbreak poured out of the wireless speakers.

"You like Adele?" Kathleen asked.

I shrugged. "She seems like a lovely person," I said.

Kathleen laughed. "But you think her music's sentimental."

"Maybe," I said. "But she's got a killer set of pipes."

Kathleen yawned, and I knew I should leave and let her sleep. But I couldn't yet. As bad as my little chat with Jamie Jordan had gone, it would have been worth it if I'd learned something useful. Why wouldn't either of them talk about that night?

"Kathleen, I have to ask you a question," I finally said.

She stared off into space, seemingly oblivious to me.

"That day on the beach, when I started bleeding," she finally said, "I was terrified. I've never been so scared in my life. I love this baby," she said. "I can't lose it now."

Her admission moved me. She must be so full of fear right now—but she still had room for love. I rocked silently for long minutes, trying to get a grip on my emotions.

"Do you trust me, Kathleen?"

Kathleen turned and smiled her lovely, innocent smile. "Of course I do. You're great. I don't know what I'd do without you."

I took a deep breath. How was it that she could knock the wind out of me with just a few little words? Was this strange charisma of hers why I was starting to believe in her?

"Kathleen, I want you to tell me about Jamie Jordan," I said gently. "I went to see him today at your high school. He said that—"

"He said we had sex," she interrupted, her voice turning bitter. "He tells people that because he thinks it's what they expect to hear. It's gross and it's pitiful. Honestly, I feel sorry for him and his lame macho fantasy."

Brave words, but I could tell Kathleen was trying to mask her hurt. "That's generous of you," I said.

"We didn't have sex. Jamie took me to Sachuest Point because he was hoping to get lucky there. But I wouldn't do more than kiss him. He was furious at me. He was like a crazy animal. But I didn't do anything else with him. That's everything there is to tell right now," she said.

I don't know what my expression was, but my mind was whirling.

"Don't you believe me?" Kathleen asked. "Please believe me, Anne. If no one believes—what will happen to me? What will happen to my baby?"

I shushed her, then got up and smoothed her hair and tucked her covers up under her chin. She'd said she was innocent, repeatedly, but it nagged at me that she always added, "That's all I can say right now."

I wanted to believe she was being honest because I cared about her so much. But...I couldn't, not quite. Something important had happened to Kathleen that night at Sachuest Point. I had been sent to Newport to find out what it was.

So far, I hadn't succeeded.

46

Newport.

As his car rolled along the drive, Nicholas Rosetti knew he'd never been more afraid for his life, or his soul.

He was about to see the second virgin.

This intense fear had begun, not during the plane crash or its horrifying aftermath, but during his meeting with Monsignor Bernard Stingley hours before. The older priest was his former mentor at the Lateran in Rome, but the gladness Rosetti had felt upon seeing him again was quickly smothered by dread.

The Voice—laughing, cackling obscenely. *You stupid, stupid fool. This vain old man can't help you. No one can help you.*

Stingley said, "I think I know why you've come, Nicholas. I have a bad feeling." He shook his head and sighed. "I've had it for weeks, actually."

Nicholas Rosetti didn't waste time. "Monsignor," he said, "I *know* that you know the secret of Fátima. Before he passed, God rest his soul, Pius told me you'd actually read the words. The message of the Virgin: the promise *and* the warning."

The monsignor didn't speak. His eyes showed nothing. He merely listened.

Rosetti continued, but suddenly he wasn't so sure about his old friend. "You were with Pius much of the time he was ill. He spoke of the secret of Fátima, and you were there to hear it all. And now I know what you know."

Distress flared in Monsignor Stingley's eyes. "Pius had no right. No right to ask you to do this. Your soul—"

"It's too late for recriminations or regrets," Rosetti said. "I know about the two virgins. One good. One evil."

"You know nothing, Nicholas." His mentor dropped his head into his hands. "There is so much more...."

Rosetti spoke fast. "Please, I need to know how to prepare myself. The search for the true virgin. What do you mean, *I know nothing?* Monsignor," he said desperately, "I want you to tell me exactly how it's going to be. I fear that my descent into Hell has already begun."

IT HAS, NICHOLAS. You have that much figured out correctly. You're already lost! Your soul is forfeited!

The Voice screamed laughter inside Rosetti's head. Then it fractured into hundreds of shrieking voices. The pain was unbearable, as if his skull were being ripped apart.

The old priest stood suddenly, overturning his chair with a resounding crash.

"They're *here!* You've brought them here!" His eyes widened in fear. "The legions are here! They're everywhere! Look beyond the two virgins, Father. Look beyond the virgins! The legions are right before your eyes."

Rosetti tried to go to him, but his arms and legs wouldn't move, as if they were weighted down by stones. He watched as the old man's skinny legs buckled and he fell to his knees. His eyes rolled upward and foam boiled over his lips and down the knob of his chin. His hands pawed the air as he fought wildly against unseen forces.

With extraordinary effort, Nicholas Rosetti lurched from his seat and fell to the floor. He crawled on his hands and knees to where Bernard Stingley lay stricken.

"Monsignor, no! Dear God, no!" And then, to the demons, "Get away from him! Take me!"

The old man whispered, but the whisper was like a roar: *"You will be taken and damned to eternity in Hell. Do you comprehend eternity? Look beyond the virgin girls. The answer is there!"*

And in that instant of terror and pain, Father Nicholas Rosetti believed that he did understand something.

He was with the legions now, and they were Hell, and they had come up from the abyss of fire to Earth.

Monsignor Stingley was screaming at the top of his voice. "Get them off me! Please, please! They're eating me alive!"

47

Kathleen felt totally spooked. Even though nothing had changed from yesterday or the day before, she felt an intense pressure building up inside her. She sensed—in a deep, wordless way, the way animals sensed earthquakes—that something bad was creeping toward Sun Cottage and everyone who lived there, especially anyone who tried to help her.

Unable to sleep, she threw back the gauzy pink curtains of her bedroom window. All she saw was the reflection of her own face in the black windowpane.

Then, through the film her breath made on the glass, she saw gold lights pricking through the dark: the carriage lamp lining the driveway casting a fuzzy glow along Ocean Avenue.

A couple of private security guards in dark parkas and baseball caps kept watch by the front gate. For some reason, their presence didn't make her feel at all secure.

A sudden movement caught her eye.

Directly below her window, a car door opened and a man got out.

He wore a black suit and a black hat with the brim severely pointed down; he held a bulging black satchel under his arm.

He looked ancient and ominous.

Even from above, Kathleen could see how stoop-shouldered he was, as if he were carrying a mountain of stone on his back.

Then she had a very odd thought: *They are here for me*. Plural.

They are here.

Voices boomed out as the front door opened and Father O'Carroll strode onto the veranda. Kathleen was surprised to see him extend his hand warmly to the dark figure. But that was when Kathleen knew who the man was.

He was the other investigator.

The priest from Rome.

Just before he entered Sun Cottage, he looked up toward her window.

Kathleen shuddered. *He looked right into my eyes,* she thought. *He already knows the truth, but he doesn't have the faith to believe it.*

48

Father Rosetti had finally arrived. Now there were three of us watching over Kathleen, trying to get at the truth. Was his presence a sign that I had failed?

Had I?

A meeting of the minds had been called in one of the handsome double parlors on the first floor of Sun Cottage. I took my place in a straight-backed chair and told myself that right now, it was my job to stay calm and listen. But my heart was thumping in double time for Kathleen.

She sat beside me in an armchair, looking tired—and frankly, ready to burst. I hoped she wouldn't be too afraid when the time came.

Charles Beavier offered drinks all around. When he got no takers, he poured himself a large scotch. Carolyn looked faint—like she could use a stiff drink herself. Justin, his expression unreadable, stood next to the sliding oak doors.

Everyone was quiet, waiting to hear what the priest from Rome had to say. He knew things that we didn't.

He was a formidable presence: alien and mysterious, dressed in black, like some eighteenth-century undertaker. I watched him anxiously clasp and unclasp his large workman's hands.

He finally smiled, but it didn't look genuine.

There was no way Father Rosetti was as in control as he'd have us believe, though he calmly greeted us in a sibilant, heavily accented voice.

Then he strode to the center of the room and took a wide-legged stance in front of Kathleen.

"My child, I have been sent here by the Vatican," Rosetti said. "For what it is worth, my official title is Chief Investigator for the Congregation of Sacred Rites. This is the body within the Church that investigates miracles, claims of sainthood, and all varieties of supernatural phenomena."

"I guess you've come to the right place, then," Kathleen said dryly.

I was surprised to see the broad-faced priest smile. "You need not be afraid of me, Kathleen. I'm something of a pushover. In spite of the theatrical title, I'm a bureaucrat. Like a tax investigator of the supernatural."

Kathleen shook her head. "I'm not afraid of you, Father."

I was glad to hear her say this, but I was concerned for her. She looked pale and tired. I was afraid she might go into labor at any moment.

Father Rosetti seemed not to notice. He was not the pushover he claimed to be. "Kathleen, is the Blessed Virgin Mary here with us tonight?" He asked this as if he were requesting the time of day. As if the answer didn't really matter to him.

Kathleen took a deep breath and pushed back a wisp of silken-blond hair.

"She's here. Yes," she said in a soft voice.

"Inside the house? In this very room with us?"

"Yes. *Right inside* this room, Father. Are you surprised? Don't you believe in the Blessed Mother?"

"I'm sorry, Kathleen," said Rosetti. His hands were working again, clenching and unclenching. "I suppose I am not used to having Our Blessed Mother quite so nearby. Is she quite beautiful? Is she standing, Kathleen? Or is she sitting over on that blue chair, perhaps?"

"Father Rosetti," Kathleen said. "I know what you're doing, but please don't try to play tricks. Our Lady is here with us. You do believe in her, don't you?"

"Kathleen, I'm concerned only with what you believe," the Vatican priest said.

There was an edge to his voice. I heard it. And I saw his facial muscles twitch.

There was no longer any doubt in my mind. The Vatican priest was absolutely terrified of Kathleen Beavier.

Why was he afraid of Kathleen?

What did he know that we didn't?

What was he here to investigate?

49

Father Rosetti paced in a tight circle at the center of the long room, ignoring all of us watching him and wondering what in the world was going on. The air seemed charged with energy, and from the twitching and fidgeting I saw around me, it seemed like I wasn't the only one to feel that way.

Rosetti, relentlessly circling, drew our gaze like a magnet. Then suddenly he stopped, dark eyes ablaze.

"I have extraordinary news," he said.

It was apparent to me that he'd dismissed all of us but Kathleen. He fastened his eyes on her.

"One of the things I have uncovered thus far, one of the few things I'm truly sure about," the chief investigator said, "is that, Kathleen, you are not alone. There are *two* virgins."

I gasped in disbelief. But Kathleen didn't move—she didn't even blink in surprise. Her face was utterly serene.

"I sensed that there were two of us. *At least two.*" Kathleen's voice was so quiet that I had to strain to hear her. She looked as if she'd fallen into a trance. "Everything is happening in great numbers right now. Plagues, droughts, deaths. And even virgins." A flicker of a smile passed over her face. "These are scary days."

The Vatican priest's eyes narrowed. "How did you know that, Kathleen? You must tell me everything that you know." He loomed over her and then grabbed the arms of her chair. *"Tell me now,"* he demanded.

But Charles Beavier, who had been silently simmering all this time, suddenly boiled over in rage. "Don't ever talk that way to my daughter!" he yelled. In two paces he was on the bulky Vatican priest, hands reaching for his neck.

I yelled "Stop!" as Justin tried to drag him off Father Rosetti's flailing body. There was a struggle—Charles thrashing, threatening to throw the priest out of the house, the priest merely trying to fend him off.

Finally Justin wedged himself between the two men, and Charles stepped back. As his wife and daughter watched, open-mouthed, he shook himself off and settled back down onto the couch.

"Enough with the third degree," Charles Beavier said, his voice shaking. "How about answering a question for me? Let's cut the investigator crap. What's your business here? Why are you in our house trying to scare us to death?"

I shot a startled glance at Justin, who returned my look of alarm.

Kathleen leaned forward in her chair. Her wide blue eyes went from me to the priest to her father. "I can answer that, Daddy," she said. "Father Rosetti has come here to find out which of us two girls is the true virgin."

50

I tossed and turned for several hours that night, trying to comprehend the news that there were *two* pregnant virgins. What could it possibly mean to the Church? And then, after I'd finally fallen asleep (though no closer to understanding *anything*), I was awakened by a persistent knocking on my bedroom door. It was 4:30 a.m.

Twelve kinds of emergencies jumped into my mind as I scrambled out of bed and flung open the door, only to find a tidied-up and smiling version of Father Rosetti standing in the hall.

"What's happened? Is Kathleen all right?" I asked.

"Good morning," he said.

"Morning?" I said incredulously.

"Sorry to get you up so early," he said, obviously not meaning the apology. "Kathleen is still sleeping, *come un angioletto.* Like the proverbial baby."

He was, he said, calling a meeting. What could I do but agree to it?

By five o'clock I'd joined Justin and the Vatican priest in the library. From the look of things, it seemed like the two of them had been up for a while.

Justin told me what he'd learned so far. "The so-called second virgin is a young girl in Ireland. Her name is Colleen. Sounds a bit like Kathleen, doesn't it? The Church is struggling to keep her situation a secret. That's easier there than over here. Father Rosetti has questioned her—"

"But I would very much like another opinion," Rosetti broke in. "And without question, you are the two people most qualified to give it. You know Kathleen and can make a comparison. Cardinal Rooney and the Vatican agree. They also think it wise to keep our circle small."

That certainly woke me up. What was he saying? That we were to fly off to Ireland to meet this girl? But what about Kathleen? And Jamie Jordan? What about the mysterious night at Sachuest Point? My investigation was in Newport, not Ireland.

As if the priest had read my mind, he said, "I've already spoken to the cardinal in Boston. I'll stay here with Kathleen and wait for your return. Go quickly. You will be back in plenty of time."

The unspoken words *"for the baby"* seemed to hang in the air.

Justin and I exchanged glances. I was thinking that I didn't particularly like this priest from Rome. Nor did I trust him. I cared about Kathleen, though, and I had a lot of work to do here in Newport. I was not going to get on a plane.

Then Rosetti did something that surprised me. He completely humbled himself. "Please. I truly need your help," he said. "There is so very much at stake...for so many people around the world. And I cannot do this job alone. Please, my friends. *You have to help me.*"

My heart turned over in that instant. I've never been able to resist an honest plea.

"All right, we'll go," I said, and Justin nodded.

Rosetti's relief was tangible. He smiled again, and I realized with a visceral shock that he wasn't nearly as old as I'd thought. He was in his late thirties; forty, tops. But something had aged him quickly and prematurely. What had he seen before he came to Newport, and what did he know that we still didn't? What were Justin and I about to see in Ireland? Would we be in danger? I thought about my gun and wondered if I should pack it.

"I think you will find Colleen Galaher extremely interesting. She has many of the same qualities you see in Kathleen," Rosetti said. "Go and you will see. Please, go. They could be sisters."

51

Less than twelve hours later, we were in Ireland, and I was trying my best to focus on a whole new set of problems.

I'd said good-bye to Kathleen and her parents, and I'd also spoken to Cardinal Rooney, who asked me to cooperate with Rome as much as I could. So here I was...about to meet the second virgin, wondering what it all could possibly mean. And I was carrying my gun.

We scooted down a country lane in a tiny little car on the wrong side of the road. Justin drove, whistling softly. He was glad to be back in the land of his birth, despite our strange and nerve-racking mission.

I tried to take comfort in his happiness as I marveled at the stark, solemn beauty of the countryside. But mostly, I couldn't help feeling afraid. Too many bad things had happened already.

After nearly two hours of driving through low hills glowing

in a hundred different shades of green, we came to a wooden road marker for the town. Next to the town's name, GOD'S COUNTRY was printed in bold black letters. At another time, the irony of the words would have made me smile.

Turning down a narrow paved lane, we passed a crowd of villagers: a dozen men all dressed in earthy brown suits, wool caps, and worn-in work boots.

Twelve pairs of eyes casting suspicious stares at our car as we drove by.

"I feel like I just time-traveled," I said. "Is it 1915 around here?"

Justin laughed. "Basically," he said. "You have now entered Maam Cross, the place where time stood still."

He turned down the main street, which was lined with small stores painted in bright colors. Soot-stained advertising posters hung loosely on the walls: PLAYER'S PLEASE cigarettes and GUINNESS FOR GREATNESS. A livery stable and garage shared a single building. Behind that stretched a row of stone cottages, freshly thatched, with their shutters newly painted.

"It's charming," I said, meaning *It's strange and lovely and* totally *foreign*.

Justin smiled. "It's great—if you don't have to live here forever." He went on to explain that each of the cottages would have a ten-by-ten-foot family room filled with knickknacks, a television, and pictures of the Virgin Mary and the Sacred Heart of Jesus. The bedrooms would be cramped and tiny. Everything would be badly lit and perfumed with the heavy smell of a turf fire.

"Sounds just like the New Jersey suburbs," I said. "All you have to do is supersize everything and exchange turf fires for Glade PlugIns."

"Touché," Justin laughed. But his laugh was cut short when we saw the graffiti on the new tea shop in the center of town.

The letters were angry red brushstrokes high up against a freshly whitewashed wall: *Colleen sucks fairie dicks!*

"Ah, that explains everything," Justin said, and smirked as we zoomed on ahead.

52

The Galaher house was about a mile and a half east of town, on a small country road, but Justin and I found it immediately, almost as if we'd been there before.

I kept feeling like none of this was in our control, and it scared me. So did the newspapers, which still carried stories of famine in India, Ebola in Egypt, and the polio outbreak back home.

As we pulled up to the gate, clouds snuffed out the sun, casting the tiny thatched and whitewashed cottage into gloom. Dying geraniums in tin-can planters nodded their faded blooms in the breeze, and a handful of chickens scattered as we climbed out of the car. There was nothing welcoming here.

But here we were in Ireland, about to meet the second virgin. I felt almost weak with anticipation and awe.

"Colleen's father passed three years ago," Justin said. "After which her mother had a stroke. She's not in her right mind anymore, and she's in her bed most days. It's not the best situation for the girl. It's certainly not like life at the Beaviers'."

"Kathleen's life isn't an easy one," I said, feeling a little defensive for some reason. "Not anymore it isn't."

"I know that, Anne," Justin said. "And Kathleen is a lovely girl. Lucky for her, the silver spoon she was born with didn't choke her. But now we have to focus on Colleen. We have a lot to learn."

"Like how the Church in Ireland has been able to keep this a secret?" I said.

Justin shrugged. "That's no surprise to me. I know the Irish Church. If Jesus Christ Himself had been born on this island, the word still might not be out."

He pushed open the rusting iron gate and it creaked under his hand. At that exact moment, the blue-painted cottage door swung open, and a large, severe-looking nun stood there before us.

"I'm Sister Katherine Dominica," she announced curtly. "Who might you be?"

We introduced ourselves, and the nun nodded her head. "We've been expecting you," she acknowledged, but she eyed us distrustfully as she showed us inside.

It was dim inside the cottage, and cold despite the fire in the grate. There was movement in the corner. A girl stood up from a low stool to greet us.

She wore a printed housedress under a frayed lace apron. Her striking dark red hair fell in thick waves down her back.

"Hello!" she said, her voice warm and welcoming—unlike the nun's. "I'm so glad you're here. It means the Church believes in me."

It was almost as if the sunshine lacking outside had materialized right here. The smile on Colleen Galaher's face actually illuminated the dreary interior of the cottage.

I gaped at her—there was no other word for it. She was radiant. She had clear ivory skin, bright green eyes, and that lovely red hair. She was a beautiful girl—a beautiful girl who was hugely pregnant.

Sixteen years old, I thought. *A child herself.*

But hadn't Mary of Nazareth given birth to Jesus at fourteen? That was the agreed-upon age.

"Could I get tea for anyone?" the girl asked in a sweet, shy voice. "Some soda bread or biscuits after your long journey from America?"

I liked Colleen Galaher instantly. Who wouldn't? And that made me feel as if I were betraying Kathleen.

No wonder Father Rosetti needed help, I thought. This was an impossible problem.

Both girls seemed perfect.

53

Colleen immediately impressed on us that she wanted to cooperate in any way she could. She had been praying that the Church would send someone.

After our tea, we walked with her single file down a thin, muddy path that twisted along behind the Galaher cottage, an uneven seam in the otherwise bright green countryside. She said it was a good place to talk, and to *listen*.

"It's very pretty out here," I said.

"Thank you, miss," she said. "I think it is, too. People around here say that it's God's country."

Justin, bringing up the rear of our party, grunted. I turned around, and he smiled grimly at me.

"So, Colleen," I said, "what do you have to say to us?"

"What do you want to know?" she asked in the softest, sweetest voice.

Is she a little too good to be true? I wondered. But wasn't that true of Kathleen as well?

Two perfect girls—a perfect puzzle.

"Why don't you just start at the beginning," I suggested. "What's the first thing that you remember...pertaining to the pregnancy?"

She nodded. "I can tell you that one. It was probably too late to be out alone," she said, "but I often come to Liffey Glade by myself. That's what I did on the night it all began."

Fields became sparse woodland, then dense thicket. When the gloom was thick around us, we came to a clearing within the trees.

Colleen pointed to a flat rock jutting out over the edge of a small stream. "I was right over there," she said, "watching the moonlight glinting on the water, when I heard their voices."

"Who did you hear, Colleen?" Justin asked. "What voices?"

A shadow crossed the young girl's face, as if her peace of mind had been breached by an ugly memory.

"It was two men and a boy around that bend," she said. "I thought they were trapping rabbits. Or maybe fishing in the stream. I called out—and it startled them. But they weren't hunting. They were doing something wrong," said the girl, her voice catching. "They didn't want me to see."

"What kind of wrong?" I asked. "What were the men doing?"

Colleen coughed, then cleared her throat. Her voice became a nervous whisper. "They had their pants down to the ground and one of them—a man as big as a bear—had his mouth on the boy... down there. The boy is in my school. The other man was someone I knew. A priest from another town. He was watching."

Colleen started to cry, and she pushed the tears away with the back of her small hand.

"The priest recognized me and began to come at me. So I ran.

And they chased me. I could hear them breathing right behind me. I ran as fast as I could.

"The bigger man grabbed me by the waist and he pulled me down. The priest covered my mouth and nose so that I couldn't scream—there was no air to breathe! Then it seemed like there were so many of them, not just the two men and the boy. It seemed like there were twenty or thirty, more than I could count.

"Then there was a loud cracking, louder than the loudest thunder. Big daggers of light turned the sky yellow and white.

"The men vanished—however many there were. They just scrambled up the scree, leaving me lying there, scraped up and bleeding. Then the rains came."

Colleen pointed across the clearing, to where an enormous oak was split in two. Half of the tree still stood, while the other half lay on the ground. I could see the fire marks that had scorched the length of the trunk.

"They didn't get me," said the young girl fervently. "The stories about me are all lies. I got away from them untouched. I am a virgin, I swear it," Colleen said, cupping her belly with both hands.

"So how did this happen to me? How could it be?" she asked us.

As we stood in the gloaming in this fairy glen, I noticed the same pinkish glow that I'd sometimes seen emanating from Kathleen now shining faintly around this girl. Could Justin see it? Could it be a nimbus?

I turned to him and saw to my shock that tears were flowing down his face. He could see the glow, too. My God, what did it mean? What was the strange light?

"If you don't believe me, ask my doctor," Colleen said. "He's right here in Maam Cross. He'll tell you the truth."

I believed her. I believed every word. And so did Justin.

And we didn't need another doctor's testimony.

Early yesterday morning, Father Rosetti had pressed Colleen's dossier into my hands. It included the medical report from a hospital in Dublin. At the Vatican's behest, they had sent a doctor to examine Colleen.

I'd read the report myself. So had Justin.

Colleen Galaher was eight and a half months pregnant.

And she was definitely a virgin.

"Please help me," she whispered. "I'm a good girl."

54

Portsmouth, Rhode Island.

I t was half past eight—prime time at the local dive bar—and Jamie Jordan wasn't half as drunk as he wanted to be. He ordered three more beers and an order of tater tots and walked back to the table where his friends sat watching the New York Giants pulverize the New England Patriots.

From the slippery looks Chris and Peter gave him, he knew that his dear pals had been talking about the night at Sachuest Point. Again. That royally pissed him off. He put his fists on the table and glared at them.

"I told you that we don't talk about that night. That means you *don't talk about it*. Especially while I'm up there ordering you dickheads beers."

Chris Raleigh rolled his dark eyes. "Don't be a paranoid asshole, Jordan. Are you wasted or something? You're acting messed up."

Jamie Jordan felt his face grow hot. "Thompson, were you talking about that night or what?"

Peter Thompson shrugged. "Dude, relax."

Jamie leaned forward threateningly. "I asked you a goddamn question."

Peter hesitated. The three of them had been inseparable since their grammar-school days in Newport, and he'd never seen Jamie so agitated. It wasn't just right now at the bar—it was always. *Everything* got to him.

"I'm waiting for your answer," Jamie said. The veins in his forehead bulged out against bone and seemed to throb.

"We *need* to talk about it, dude. This whole thing has gotten out of hand. In case you haven't fucking noticed," Peter said. "We need to do something. We need a plan."

Without thought or warning, Jamie Jordan hit his friend hard in the chest with a closed fist. Peter reeled off his chair and fell down onto the sticky linoleum floor.

The bartender was on them in an instant. "You little shits cut the crap here or I'm calling the cops." He smiled with nicotine-stained teeth. "After I kick your collective fake-ID asses."

The room went quiet. The barflies glared toward the commotion in the corner.

"Boot 'em, Rick," called an old drunk.

Jamie Jordan clenched his fists. He was *this close* to taking a swing at the bartender. But then he spun away and lunged toward the front door.

Outside, with the sea breeze whipping across his face, Jamie Jordan thought about going right back in. He'd take down the bartender and then wipe the floor with Thompson and Raleigh. Oh, Christ! He smacked his palm hard. Kathleen Beavier was the one he ought to beat down.

He'd practically had to get down on his knees and beg the Ice Queen for a date. He'd driven over to the Catholic high school to meet her getting out of class on ten different afternoons. He'd washed his car, worn his best clothes, and sweated over the music cued up on his iPhone.

There was something different, something special, about Kathleen Beavier, he had to admit. He'd wanted her more than he'd ever wanted any girl. Of course he wanted to fuck her, but he also just wanted to be *around* her. She had *it*. He'd even thought that he loved her.

Until that night at Sachuest Point.

Where something really bad had happened.

55

Jamie Jordan fired up the motor of his Mercedes SL550 and turned the music on full volume. Screw his fucktard friends—they could find their own way home. As he jerked the yellow sports car out onto the road, he yelled out the words to a Chris Brown song.

Maybe he *was* drunk after all. Maybe he was totally wasted.

And he hadn't gotten his fucking tater tots.

As he drove up the steep cobblestoned hill behind the bar, he thought back to the night of February 23, when he'd taken Kathleen to the St. Mary's dance. Jamie's parents had plenty of money, but he'd still felt intimidated as he drove up to the Beavier house that night. He'd worn a tux and he knew he looked great, but for some reason he felt nervous. Charles Beavier had answered the front door in the middle of a phone call and invited him in with only a nod.

So Jamie stood like an idiot in the foyer. Mrs. Beavier didn't appear and Mr. Beavier was busy reading someone the riot act via cell phone. He checked his bow tie in the gilded mirror and thought about taking a selfie, because standing in this fancy hallway, he looked like a damn aristocrat. He was just pulling out his phone when Kathleen appeared.

The sight of her had taken his breath away. She had on a shimmery, slim dress the color of sea foam. She wore a silver headband in her shining blond hair. She was so beautiful it almost hurt to look at her. She looked like royalty, he thought.

He'd expected the St. Mary's dance to be awful, but it was even worse than he'd thought it could be. The band was a middle-aged blues quartet that played at all of the Newport club and debutante teas. Flocks of nuns watched over the dance like hawks, making sure the couples kept six inches of airspace between their bodies.

He'd been desperate to leave after the first five minutes. But Kathleen seemed to like it, and maybe she was worth all this torture.

There was supposed to be a party after the dance, too. Kathleen had shown him an invitation embossed on thick ivory paper: *Come to an after-party at Elaine Scaparella's house.*

She'd pressed against him when the nuns weren't looking, tantalizing him with her faint perfume and the delicious hint of cleavage showing below her neckline. And when she put her head on his shoulder during the last dance, he could almost taste her. He wanted her so bad, and he knew she wanted him, too.

It had been easy to talk her into skipping the dumb party and going for a ride along Second Beach to Sachuest Point.

But now he wished to God that they had never gone there. He wished he had never laid eyes, or especially hands, on Kathleen Beavier.

56

As Jamie headed out past Second Beach now, the high beams of his Mercedes stabbed through thick autumnal fog. He felt pretty wasted, but his driving was okay. This wasn't the first time he'd been shit-faced behind the wheel of a car.

He was driving back to Sachuest Point—where he'd taken Kathleen almost nine months before on the night that changed both of their lives.

Something bad *had* happened out there. Something crazy.

He knew it.

So did Thompson and Raleigh.

And so did Kathleen, that phony bitch. That goddamn liar.

Jamie didn't know why he was going back. It wasn't like he wanted to relive that hell. But it seemed like it was out of his hands—as if he just *had* to go there tonight.

As he banked the sports car around a soft S-curve, he noticed his vision tunneling. Strange as hell. He shook his head to clear it. A dull, throbbing ache that began near his left ear moved up to behind his eyes.

Oh, Jesus, not again, Jamie thought.

He looked down at the Mercedes' dashboard. The car's glowing clock read 9:54. The speedometer was at 60-plus. And the ringing was starting.

Shit. Soon he'd feel a painful pounding at the top of his skull. Simultaneous noise and pain. He knew what to expect.

Memorial Boulevard became a ruler-straight two-lane blacktop as it approached Sachuest Point. In his rearview mirror Jamie could see the receding lights of southeastern Newport and the glittery mansions on the coast.

He had a sudden desire to take the car over the point. It would be so easy—like flying.

God, what was wrong with him? He frowned and shook his head painfully. What kind of crazy thought was that? His car was badass—but he knew the damn thing couldn't fly.

Another unwanted thought circled and then intruded. *Kathleen.* And a shrill banshee wail started up in his brain.

Just remembering that night made him feel so awful. But he couldn't turn back the clock. And the next day, too, when he told everyone. "Yo, I popped a St. Mary's cherry," he'd said, and then he'd high-fived his bros like they'd just won a lacrosse game.

Jamie reached up and touched his head. The pain was so intense he felt nauseated.

That was why he wanted to cut the wheel—cut it *now*—cut it into the concrete retaining wall.

Tires screamed. Rubber fused to asphalt.

He put both hands on the steering wheel and forced the car back to the center of the road. He was going crazy, that was it. The top of his head was going to blow off. And still the pain kept growing.

171

Then stop the pain, he heard. *You can do it, you know. You're in control. Besides, you deserve to die, and you know it. For what you did.*

The yellow Mercedes swerved to the left and crossed the double yellow stripes again. The steering wheel didn't feel solid anymore. He couldn't grip it. His hands flew off the wheel and he covered his ears.

See, you can do it! You can fly. YOU CAN FLY!

The sports car shot out of control, just missing an oncoming Jeep. *God, that was close.*

Blue-white headlights blinded him for a second. An angry car horn trailed off into the thickening fog.

He held on tightly as his car continued its irresistible skid on the slick black road. Suddenly he *was* flying. The front wheels left the ground, and the world seemed to go silent.

The car's headlamps pointed toward the constellation of Orion before illuminating the downward curve of the car's trajectory.

He wasn't flying anymore. He was falling.

Jamie Jordan screamed, but only the seagulls heard it: "I'm sorry, Kathleen! Oh, God, I'm so sorry!"

57

Kathleen sat up in bed; something was terribly wrong.

The clock on her nightstand said that it was 11:24. Then 11.25, then 11.26. The numbers clicked forward inexorably, but Kathleen couldn't sleep.

I don't want you to sleep, she heard the Voice say. *You'll never sleep again. And that's not good for the baby, is it?*

Her cell phone rang.

As she'd known it would.

Her hand slid slowly out from under the warm covers that sloped over the mound of her stomach and reached for the phone. It was her friend Sara. "Um…hello?" she whispered.

Kathleen heard a hiccup, and then a sob. Then Sara's voice sounding horribly far away. "Oh, honey, I'm so sorry," Sara said.

"Sara, what is it? Sorry about what? What's going on?"

"Jamie's dead, Kathleen," Sara sobbed. "He was drinking, and he drove his car off Sachuest Point."

Shocked, Kathleen put down the phone.

She got out of bed and tugged on her maternity jeans and an oversized sweatshirt. She felt like she might throw up, and she didn't know if it was pregnancy or grief.

She was heartsick.

The house creaked like an old ship under her feet as she slipped into the dimly lit anteroom that led to her father's bedroom. His door was ajar, and she could hear him snoring softly. His keys lay in a brass bowl on his desk.

She picked them up, and as quietly as she could, she hurried downstairs. She grabbed her navy-blue parka off the coat hook.

She had to go see about Jamie.

She had an awful feeling that somehow this was her fault.

58

Kathleen drove her father's Lincoln down a gravel road that ran parallel to the sand, then twisted out of the beach bramble half a mile south of the main house.

She was throbbing inside. Her eyes blurred with tears as she headed down Ocean Avenue, now slick with rain. The beachside road was like a twisting ribbon of shiny black glass. She was doing everything she could not to crash herself, but the desire to make everything go away was so incredibly intense.

But she had more at stake here than her own life. She had to keep the baby safe.

So Kathleen kept both hands rigidly clasped on the steering wheel and her eyes fastened on the bold yellow center stripe of the road.

As she drove, she began to remember what had happened that night in February.

It was finally coming back to her. She was so close to the truth. . . .

But then she lost it again, like always.

Damn it! Damn it! Damn!

She arrived at Sachuest Point a little past 11:45.

"Oh my God," she whispered.

The bleak, bald hillside that marked the beginning of the wildlife preserve was illuminated by the headlights of a long procession of cars coming from town. Newport and Portsmouth police vehicles were parked helter-skelter all over the hill. Kathleen heard the distant roar of an approaching helicopter.

She knew exactly where to go. This was where it had happened. This was where it all started in February.

She could almost remember—but it kept fading away.

She was blocking it. She knew she was.

But why?

A freezing wet wind sliced up from the ocean. Waves crashed like thunder on the rocks just beyond the roadside, and a thick bluish-gray fog lay over the entire area.

A crowd had gathered. People were craning their necks to get a better look at the accident. She was elbowing her way past the knot of onlookers to the site of the wreck when the Newport city police chief recognized her. He shook his head no.

"I have to go down there," Kathleen said. "I have to. I'm going."

Captain Walker Depew took off his black-visored cap and nervously thumped it against his leg.

"It's not a good idea, Ms. Beavier. It's a terrible scene down there. James Jordan is dead. I'm sorry."

Kathleen choked back a sob and pushed past the flustered police chief as if he weren't there. Peering through the fog, she could see where the yellow Mercedes had struck the rocks, grille first.

As if hypnotized, she put one foot in front of the other. One hand on her stomach, the other bracing against the rocks, she began the tricky descent.

Your lover is dead! She heard a voice screech inside her head. *It's time to admit the truth about you and Jamie. Tell the truth, you bitch!*

Kathleen wanted to do it—but she couldn't remember what had happened.

"I don't know what happened!" she whispered through gritted teeth. *"I don't remember."*

A murmur rose and spread back among the crowd gathered on the road.

"It's her! The virgin."

"Hail Mary, full of grace!" A woman's voice rang out in the fog and drizzle.

"No, *please*," Kathleen called, waving for the prayers to stop. "Go away. Please, just go away."

She walked on toward the overturned car, lit up in a harsh blue glow coming from two police emergency lamps trained on it.

A Newport policeman, a young trooper in a black leather jacket, held out his bulky arm to stop her.

"Stop there, please, miss."

She brushed past without even glancing at his face. There was no way any of them was going to stop her. Kathleen was less than thirty feet from Jamie Jordan now. She saw the whipped foam bubbling on the car's engine, a precaution against an explosion.

She couldn't help thinking: *Two suicide attempts and now a death, all since that night in February. Am I carrying a blessing . . . or a curse?*

59

Les Porter of the *New York Daily News* sat in his rental car on a hillside in the frigid New England night, in shock that he was here to witness the latest twist in the Virgin of Newport story. His cell battery was at 6 percent, his coffee was cold, and he was nearly bursting with unanswered questions.

He wasn't alone. Word had exploded from ground zero, where the yellow Mercedes had slammed into the rocks, to the fringes of the crowd in microseconds. Before you could say "Live from Newport," television reporters and fanatics and run-of-the-mill rubberneckers rushed to the fogged-in scene of the fatal accident.

Then Kathleen Beavier had arrived. Porter had rarely witnessed a more dramatic scene in his years as a reporter. She approached the still-smoldering automobile wreck where the boy lay dead.

When she knelt to pray, a bright light suddenly appeared over the crowd. Someone in the crowd gathered along the shoreline began to scream, "Miracle! It's a miracle!"

Fanatic, Porter thought to himself.

But the strange light seemed to intensify and then take on a halo effect. Was it possible? Kathleen Beavier looked like she was *glowing.*

Porter switched on his radio and searched for his competition on the airwaves. Andrew Klauk, at WNPC in Newport, was reporting from Second Beach. Loud, interfering static preceded his report.

Finally, a crisp young male voice came through in the unmistakably self-conscious style of local radio reportage.

"Kathleen Beavier is kneeling at the scene of James Jordan's tragic accident. It seems a touching and moving gesture to everyone gathered here tonight. The young girl is approximately fifteen yards from the twisted wreckage. The Sachuest Point area is blanketed with a kind of graveyard fog, which contributes to the eeriness of the scene.

"Several people have begun to pray out loud with Kathleen Beavier. One can't help thinking of the power and glory of the ancient Church, of the role religion once played in so many lives.

"A bright light is moving right in toward the Beavier girl. People are becoming hysterical now. They seem to believe the light represents something mystical or divine. I see that a woman has fainted.

"But wait. It's something else. The light is not coming from heaven. It's coming from a boat out on the water. I have confirmation that the Castle Hill Coast Guard station's search-and-rescue boat, the *Forty-one,* has been drawn to shore by the noise and car lights. The fog covered the boat until it was up close. The light we all saw was the searchlight on the starboard side of the *Forty-one*'s cabin.

"There was *no miracle* at Sachuest Point tonight. Sadly, there was only tragedy."

Les Porter stared down the hill and watched Kathleen Beavier walk slowly away from the smoldering wreck of the boy's car.

Is all this a hoax? he thought.

Of course it was; it had to be.

60

I spotted Kathleen's girlfriends as soon as we arrived at the scene of the accident. Francesca and Sara looked hysterical with grief, but somehow Chuck was keeping herself together. Once again, they were caught behind police barricades and couldn't get anywhere near Kathleen.

"You guys all right?" I asked.

"Of course not," Francesca said, tears running down her full pink cheeks. Chuck moved to put her arm around her.

"I'll tell Kathleen you're here," I said. "I'm sure she'll be glad to know."

"He'd never kill himself, you know," Chuck said as I walked by her. "He loved himself too much."

I thought about this as I continued down the steep hill toward the wreck. What was she intimating to me? That Jamie Jordan had somehow been murdered?

Things were getting stranger by the second.

"I'm Kathleen's guardian," I said to anyone who looked like they might try to stop me on the way down. I felt like I had a right to be here.

Justin kept close behind me on the path; his story was that he was with the Archdiocese of Boston and staying with the Beaviers.

Kathleen saw us coming and she climbed the rocks toward me. I was suddenly afraid for her. The two of us hugged tightly and I could feel how hard she was shivering. Her eyes were red-rimmed and she looked as if she'd been crying for hours.

"Something really bad happened here, Anne. Not just tonight— back in February. *I can't remember!* I'm trying really hard, but I just can't. It's why Jamie died, though. Oh, Anne, Anne, it's all my fault. I'm not a holy person. I killed Jamie. What is happening to me?"

61

Dread took Kathleen Beavier into its icy grip and shook her out of deepest sleep the next morning. She nearly always woke with a sense that she had done something wrong and that she was going to be punished for it. But today, she *knew* it was true.

Jamie Jordan was dead, even if she still couldn't accept it. She'd felt his sagging weight in the body bag almost as if she were part of the EMS crew that staggered up the rocks with him. And she felt drained by the certainty that he was gone.

Outside Kathleen's window, the air shifted in the aftermath of the night's blustering storm. Leaves and branches had been ripped from the trees, and the tossing ocean still looked disturbed.

There was a faint dirty odor under everything that was hard to describe. Like a refrigerator that needed cleaning. Or old laundry left in a car trunk over the summer.

Like something was rotting.

Kathleen wondered if the odor was coming from her.

Climbing stiff-legged and off-balance from her bed, she went to her bathroom. She used the toilet and brushed her teeth. While staring at her sleep-swollen face in the mirror, Kathleen was assailed by a recurring, guilt-ridden vision.

She imagined her baby with a grotesque, twisted body and a misshapen skull. When it cried, its voice would be like a calf's being torn from its mother and dragged off to slaughter.

It was a cruel fantasy, and Kathleen believed it was just that. But because the thoughts came regularly, it was a hard fantasy to shake.

Kathleen had other doubts, too: practical concerns about what she would do after her baby was born, about what life would be like once she had her child.

When she thought of the leering crowds last night, she shuddered. They'd acted as if they owned her. First they'd called her a miracle, and then—when the light had turned out to be a Coast Guard boat—some of them had called her names.

How could she live a normal life ever again? She probably couldn't.

And she hadn't asked for this. She hadn't done anything to deserve it.

She wanted to tell everything about that night—the twenty-third of February. She'd just put it out there. *If only she could remember.*

Last night was the first time certain things had begun to come back to her. There was an image of herself in that lovely green dress. Then driving through darkness. And then a lot of men standing around her out at Sachuest Point.

It didn't seem likely, but that was what she remembered. *A lot of men circling her,* not letting her get away. And then what had happened?

Kathleen wanted to remember, but...maybe it was better that she couldn't.

184

62

Kathleen heard the pine floorboards creak sharply across her bedroom. She yelped, and then saw the face of Mrs. Walsh.

"Oh, God," she said, clutching her chest. "You scared me. Hi, Mrs. W." Then she smiled.

But there was no cheery "Good morning" from Ida Walsh. Not a word.

Kathleen's heart began to thump in her chest. Mrs. Walsh was against her, too.

She sat on the stool in front of her vanity mirror. Fumbling with her woolen socks, she began the exceedingly awkward job of getting her feet into them. She was unnerved, but she tried to tell herself that Mrs. Walsh's stony, cruel expression was just her imagination.

The upstairs part of the house was particularly quiet and still. It made things even more uncomfortable between them. The sock resisted Kathleen's efforts, and she had to stop herself from flinging it across the room. She hadn't thrown a tantrum since she was six, and she was not going to let Mrs. Walsh see her do it now.

"I'll be out of here in just a minute. Two seconds," she said, gritting her teeth.

Why isn't she talking to me? Kathleen thought.

What could I have done to her? Mrs. Walsh is more of a mother to me than my own mother!

A flicker in the mirror caught her attention.

Kathleen looked up again at the older woman. It took an impossibly long second to understand what she saw.

Ida held a gleaming blade in her hand—the lethal double-edged knife used to slice and gut fish in the Beavier kitchen.

The housekeeper let out a harsh guttural rasp—almost a bark— and then shouted, "In the name of the Holy Father, I chase out Satan and his fiendish child!"

Then she slashed down hard at Kathleen's stomach.

Reflex alone made Kathleen twist away from the flashing knife. The long blade drove deep into the wooden vanity, missing her by inches.

Kathleen jerked herself away from Ida Walsh as the crazed housekeeper furiously struggled to pull the knife free.

"Ida, stop!" she yelled from the doorway. "It's me, Kathleen! What are you doing?"

"You're not one of God's! *You're not even Kathleen!*" Ida Walsh screamed. "You are Satan's whore!"

Her face was screwed up, livid, and her eyes blazed with hate. The muscles of her arms bulged. Kathleen barely recognized the woman she'd known since the day she was born.

"Ida, no. Please. I *am* Kathleen! See, look, it's me. And my baby!"

But Ida had freed the knife and was now advancing toward her.

Kathleen gave a shriek and ran awkwardly for the stairs, rico-cheting off the doorjamb as she passed through. She caught the finial of the banister, steadied herself, and then started down the stairs as fast as she could go.

She'd gone only two steps when she felt a mighty shove at her back.

Then came the awful, terrifying feeling of weightlessness.

Kathleen screamed again, a long, looping wail, a sound she barely recognized.

She reached for the banister, but her falling weight was too much for her grasp. Her arm wrenched in the socket, and she let go.

Oh, God, no. The baby.

She fell forward, her shoulder slamming solidly into the banis-ter. Wood cracked, then gravity dragged her down.

The steep stairs were like a chute filled with boulders. Kathleen began to roll. She cracked against every step, feeling every sharp dig. Shooting pains went through her elbows and shins.

The wind went out of her as she took a powerful blow to the stomach.

Dear God! Oh, please, don't let it end like this.

Lancing pain radiated from a blow to her right ear.

Then the landing rose up and smacked her hard across her chest. She gasped for breath and struggled to rise. Levering herself up painfully, she got to her knees.

Every nerve in her body sang in agony.

Kathleen knew without looking that Ida Walsh was close. She was lumbering down the stairs, coming fast behind her, still holding the murderous knife.

"Satan!" she screeched. "He is inside you! It's Satan himself. You can't deny it any longer."

63

I had dug myself a snug windbreak among the sand dunes behind Sun Cottage, and I lay flat on a plaid wool blanket, feeling the brief and welcome appearance of late autumn sun on my face.

I breathed in the clean, crisp November air that lashed at the grasses and the dark-blue water and listened to the distant cry of a seagull.

It was glorious.

After a while, I closed my eyes and thought about Justin.

I didn't have any idea where the two of us were headed—if anywhere—but it felt like we were doing things the right way this time. I had to admit that the more I saw of him, the more irresistible he became. But I didn't know if he felt the same. Could he possibly still be in love with me? Was he questioning his vows as a priest? Or had he moved on? Were we fated always to be apart?

I listened to the distant seagull again and heard the blast of a horn from a ship. I was grateful to steal this moment away from a day of stress and uncertainty. It felt good to be alone and—even for just a moment—at peace.

The gull cried again. But this time goose bumps rose on my forearms. Something about that sound was wrong.

I got to my feet and looked around, suddenly afraid.

The cry came again.

It was a piercing screech that seemed to be coming from Sun Cottage. It went up in pitch and volume and then cut off abruptly.

And a chill snuffed out all the warmth for miles around.

The cry hadn't come from a bird.

It was *Kathleen*.

Then I saw her.

Climbing out of a window onto the roof of Sun Cottage.

64

Bruised and bleeding from her fall, Kathleen ran barefoot into a second-floor bedroom. Ida Walsh was right behind her, the knife tight in her hand and a wild, inhuman gleam in her eyes. There was no time to think: Kathleen pushed the casement window open and stepped down hard on the steep roof jutting out over the main dining room.

"You are not one of God's!" The shriek pierced Kathleen's ears. "You are Satan! I see through your tricks. Your disguise!"

"Stop it," Kathleen sobbed. "I *am* Kathleen. Ida, please, it's me!"

She tottered above the flagstone patio, her feet sliding on the cold slate shingles of the roof.

"Help! Somebody please help," she screamed, but the wind carried her voice away. Nobody seemed to hear her. *Where was everybody?*

She heard a noise behind her and she swung around to see Ida Walsh, who had squeezed through the bedroom window, now crab-walking along the steeply slanting roof. When she got within a few feet of Kathleen, she stood and tried to grab her.

"You are not Kathleen!" she bellowed, her voice lower now, almost like a man's.

Two groundsmen working below stared up at the roof in disbelief.

"Help me!" Kathleen screamed to them. "She's crazy. She has a knife!"

Protect the child became Kathleen's only thought. *Protect the child. Nothing matters but the child. Not Satan's child, either. My baby!*

The woman who had once braided her hair, said prayers with her, sung her to sleep, and loved her like her own flesh and blood had *murder* in her eyes. Where had that sweet woman gone?

"You are not Kathleen! I know Kathleen! I loved Kathleen!"

She inched across the slate even as Kathleen, hurt and ungainly, moved away from her.

Ida Walsh's eyes were wide and blank and glittering. Her white hair swirled in the wind like snow.

Kathleen finally saw Anne racing up from the beach, screaming, waving her arms wildly.

"Anne! Help me," she called down over the edge of the roof. She could easily fall now. She was so close.

She saw her mother leaning out another window, looking stricken and trying to get outside, too. Poor mom—she was never any real help. They would all be too late. There was no escape from Mrs. Walsh and her knife.

Kathleen went as far as she could, out to where the half-roof made a 90-degree turn around a corner of the house. She couldn't take another step without falling. The slate shingles slid and rattled underfoot.

Desperate, she turned and faced her attacker. "I command you to stop! I command you!" she yelled.

Ida Walsh's bare white arms stretched out for Kathleen. The knife gleamed in the sunlight. "I know the truth about you. I know your dirty secret!"

Out of the corner of her eye, Kathleen saw a flash of movement—a figure suddenly running in the driveway below. She was afraid to look away from Mrs. Walsh. She thought it might be Anne down there, but how could she help? How could anyone but God himself?

A loud noise cracked, then thundered away from Sun Cottage. Kathleen's mouth opened wide in horror.

Blood sheeted from Ida Walsh's neck. The woman swayed, the knife clattered on the shingles, and she clutched at her wound. Her face was a rictus of shock and hate. Then she dropped like a stone from the roof and slammed down onto the flagstone patio.

Everything was quiet except for the distant crash and roll of the sea.

Kathleen's eyes fell to where Anne stood. Her legs were spread in a shooter's stance. She held a pistol in front of her.

65

I wouldn't let myself go into shock; I couldn't. I thought I finally understood why I'd been sent to Sun Cottage. And I understood—the way a soldier must, when he or she is sent to war—that sometimes killing can't be avoided.

I'd thought Cardinal Rooney was making a joke when he asked me if I had a gun license. Now I knew better.

I wasn't here just to investigate Kathleen; I was here to protect her.

It was getting harder and harder not to believe in something. In Kathleen? In Colleen? In good? In evil? My mind reeled. I had shot a sixty-two-year-old woman named Ida Walsh. She had a husband. A Corgi. And thanks to me, she now had a gaping hole in her neck, through which her lifeblood had spilled onto a family's driveway. The family she cared for and loved for twenty years.

It was horrifying. I felt like I understood evil in a new way.

Kathleen and I sat huddled together on the antique glider in the sunroom, staring blindly at the choppy sea.

I was rocking a still-tearful Kathleen in my arms when I heard the phone ring downstairs. Now what? The Newport police had already been out here to question me. EMS workers had taken away the body of Mrs. Walsh.

I killed her. How could it have happened?

Just before one o'clock, Father Rosetti called another of his meetings. The Beavier family, Justin, and I gathered in the library, where Rosetti revealed that he had received orders from Rome a short time ago. Kathleen, along with a small entourage, was to leave Newport immediately. Sun Cottage was no longer safe, he said (which was hardly news to me). But was anywhere safe?

At one thirty, three black Lincoln sedans pulled up under the elegant porte cochere at Sun Cottage. Before the front gate could swing shut, a horde of shouting journalists began running up the long driveway.

On signal, seven of us were escorted out of the house and into the three waiting cars.

Windows up, doors locked, seat belts cinched, our small caravan shot toward the gate and streamed off the estate, accompanied by the police escort's penetrating sirens. We sped right past the surprised reporters.

We made it to Route 24, and moments later we hit eighty-plus miles per hour. I turned to look behind us. Vans stuffed with frantic newspeople were only a few car lengths away.

I hung on to the armrest and prayed that Kathleen, who was in another car, would be safe. I worried that the bumps and twists in the road would make her go into labor. Or that a tiny wrench of the wheel could send the car careening into a tree.

There was a four-way intersection with a blinking yellow light up ahead, but we weren't slowing down. The three drivers, who'd been in constant radio communication, knew what to do. Or at least I hoped they did.

One car peeled off to the west, another to the east.

The third car, our car, headed north to Logan International Airport in Boston.

I settled back in my seat for the journey. But every time I shut my eyes, I kept seeing Mrs. Walsh as she fell from the roof.

"Kathleen, Kathleen," reporters yelled as they swamped our car at Logan, hemming us in to the curb.

I got out of the car and whisked off the black shawl covering my head. I tossed the pillow I'd stuffed under my dress into the backseat.

"I'm not Kathleen Beavier," I said. "Sorry." And I couldn't hold back a smile.

The reporters nearly howled their anger at this ruse. The disguise meant to throw them off Kathleen's trail had worked. They had no idea that she was boarding another plane at a different airport.

And Justin and I were traveling together again.

I would have liked to consider what this might mean to us. But my eyes grew heavy and I gave in to sleep.

We arrived at Charles de Gaulle Airport in Paris at 6:45 a.m. We'd barely set foot on the ground when I caught a glimpse of Kathleen's picture on the ubiquitous terminal TV screens.

I stopped in my tracks.

Other images flashed one after another, each more terrible than the one before: children stricken with aches and high fevers streaming to Necker Hospital in Paris. It was polio again. The epidemic had jumped the Atlantic Ocean and had launched itself against Western Europe.

I felt faint and had to sit down. I remembered what I had seen at Cedars–Sinai Medical Center in L.A.

There was no logical explanation, but children were dying. And it seemed mysteriously connected to Kathleen.

Or perhaps the child she carried.

66

Colleen Galaher awoke heavy-hearted, with a feeling that was almost nausea. Each day, each *hour*, it was getting worse, and she could neither make it go away nor explain it.

She wanted to go to confession, to cleanse her soul. She needed absolution. *Now.*

A blessing. *Now.*

She wanted to do it for the child growing inside her. She wanted to do it to honor God. To show that her love and devotion were unwavering.

To Sister Katherine, who almost never left her side anymore, she said, "I want to go to church. I want to pray. Please."

The nun frowned but agreed to let the girl go.

It was still early morning, and the low hills surrounding the Irish village of Maam Cross seemed to gleam through a misty curtain of gentle rain. On a stone wall–bordered path twisting down out of the hills, the virgin and the black-cloaked nun walked, their heads bobbing against a sea of lush green.

In half an hour, Colleen had reached the rocky crossroads at the outskirts of the village. A handful of men, gathered for the sheep market later that morning, perked up when they saw the young woman approaching.

"Is the father among us, Colleen?" one of the villagers called out.

"Won't ya at least tell us that, dearie? Who's the da?" asked another, his face hidden under a battered wool cap.

"I'd say she's ready for the Abbey Theatre, with her fine actin' performance there."

"She's no holy one," a man said, and spat onto the rocky ground. "She's a little tramp." *"A bloody little blaspheming tramp!"*

Colleen ducked her head and hurried past them. As she and the nun got a few paces down the road, a heavy stone thudded down right near their feet, kicking up a volley of dirt. It could have easily felled either of them.

"No harm intended," one of the men called, laughing. "Sticks and stones won't hurt ya."

"Ya little whore!" yelled another.

Colleen whirled around and faced the gang of men. She held her hands over her belly protectively as she glared at them. "You're all cowards!" she shouted. "Cowards and gossips. I am a good girl and always have been. And I am a *virgin!*"

The men whooped and laughed—until the air seemed to darken over their heads.

From every corner of the sky came jet-black birds. Their terrible squawks grew deafening as they massed together above the group like a living storm cloud.

The Irishmen grew silent as the dead.

67

The birds vanished as quickly and mysteriously as they had gathered, and Colleen continued into the town without further disturbance. She felt better, too. Protected.

The Church of St. Joseph's sat at the village center, immaculately tidy and surrounded by a fieldstone fence. Colleen blessed herself with holy water at the entrance font and felt her heart open to God. She ached for benediction.

The church doors opened as they arrived, and Father Flannery, the young village priest, appeared in the archway. He was new to the parish, here only a few months, and he stared at her for a long moment. She stared back. His eyes were deep blue and his black hair was combed neatly to the left. Colleen had thought him the handsomest man she had ever seen, until she met the priest from America. *Where is Father O'Carroll now?* she wondered. Where was help when she so badly needed it?

"Colleen Galaher, I'd like a word with you," the priest said gently. "Please. Come inside the rectory. It's important."

He turned and, with a nod, dismissed the nun. He showed the girl into the rectory and closed the heavy wooden door behind them.

"What is it, Father? Is it word from Rome? Do they believe me?"

Colleen's heart beat faster in the silence. She lifted her face toward the priest, anxiously awaiting his instructions. She felt wide-open, vulnerable, ready to accept God's love.

The priest reached out a long-fingered hand and grazed her cheek with it.

She flinched.

His touch seared her skin.

"You've done nothing wrong, my child. You're a beautiful, beautiful woman now. There's nothing wrong in that."

Father Flannery's other hand cupped her breast.

Colleen gasped and clasped herself across the chest. She stumbled backward against a hassock and barely caught herself from falling.

"Stop," she whispered. "You're a *priest*."

"But I love you," Father Flannery said. He was quicker than the awkward, heavily pregnant teenager. He reached for her, pulled her face toward his, and pressed his mouth against hers. Again her flesh burned at his touch, as if his lips were made of fire.

"Nooooo!"

She pulled back and stared at him. Just *stared*.

And then he began to moan.

Colleen twisted free of his grasp. She burst through the narrow doorway and out into the village square.

A small crowd had gathered, and they began to yell and jeer when they saw her.

"She has no right to be inside the church!" a woman called out. Then they all joined in. "Not in our church! Not in our church."

A young boy picked up a stone and threw it at her.

Colleen couldn't run—she was too tired, too ungainly. But she tried to hurry as she stumbled and lurched through the narrow streets.

This was so frightening and so unfair. She wondered if Mary of Nazareth had suffered the same insults and cruelty. Colleen was sure that she had. Even Joseph, Mary's betrothed, didn't believe her at first.

"I am what I say," she sobbed, "a virgin with child."

And on the way home, the birds were back in the sky again—protecting her.

68

I slumped into the deep leather backseat of the sedan. A tight fist of tension had burrowed into the small of my back, and my day-long headache was pounding behind my eyes.

I found myself thinking of Colleen Galaher marking time in her tiny cottage. Kathleen—wherever she was with Father Rosetti—was counting down the hours as well. After the births... *then what?*

As our car flashed through the countryside toward the village of Chantilly, I saw again the falling body of Ida Walsh. I never believed that I would ever kill someone—and I could still hear her final scream.

The image of her broken body was a nightmare to me. And Father Rosetti's explanation seemed nightmarish, too. "The Devil," he told me, "is irresistibly drawn to Kathleen. Anne, I don't know why that is so. Not yet. *Satanas Luciferi excelsi.*"

What did he mean by "the Devil will be exalted"? Where?

When? How? The Vatican was famous for its secrecy, and Rosetti was obviously a skilled practitioner of the art.

I didn't even know what we were doing here.

I looked up toward the front of the sedan. Thick glass separated Justin and me from the driver, a silent, thick-necked man wearing a chauffeur's cap. Who was *he?* How could we be sure that he should be trusted?

I'd begun to feel paranoid about everything. If Mrs. Walsh could suddenly become possessed, then it could happen to anyone... even to Justin or me.

Satanas Luciferi excelsi.

"What happened today was a terrible thing, but it had to be that way." Justin came out of his reverie and spoke. "If you're tearing yourself up about it, you shouldn't. You did what you had to do."

I felt myself begin to shake. "I was brought in to expose a hoax—to be a paid skeptic—but I can't do it anymore," I said. "I can't deny what I've seen with my own eyes." I took a deep, shuddering breath. "And what I've done with my own hands."

Justin rubbed his palm over a day-old beard. He had dark pouches under his eyes, and I was sure I looked no better. But I couldn't imagine anyone I'd rather be with right now.

"It's like I'm a kid again, in Cork. No adult, no one in authority, would ever answer our questions. About anything. We were always kept in the dark."

"Life must have felt pretty mysterious back then," I said, trying to smile.

"Life is mysterious," Justin said softly. "And frightening and magical and crazy... and all too short."

I reached out, took his hand, and held it until we arrived.

And I thought to myself, *The hand of a priest.*

69

I awoke with a start, unsure of where I was until I remembered that we were in France. It was dark outside, and the fog had grown thick, obscuring everything beyond the car's headlights as we sped through the French countryside.

We were going very fast, too fast, and I held on tight to Justin's arm. He barely acknowledged me, as if his mind was very far away. I took a moment to study his face and felt a sudden overwhelming surge of tenderness. I couldn't help wondering again how the two of us fit into the mystery.

We were headed to a safe house that had originally been chosen as the site of Kathleen's delivery before everything changed. It was a gentleman's farm belonging to Henri Beavier, Charles's younger brother, and we were to wait there for Father Rosetti's orders.

Rosetti and the Vatican were in charge now; that much was clear.

The car slowed as it approached a high privet hedge, and then it stopped just outside large black iron gates. I was relieved we'd finally arrived, but even that small burst of joy was tinged with anxiety. The large villa, looming above the dark grounds, seemed cold and forbidding.

The gates swung inward, and as they did, a white van materialized out of the fog to our left, brakes screeching. It stopped, and the sliding doors slammed open.

I saw electric blue lettering on the van's side: GDZ-TV.

It was an ambush.

Cameramen with minipacks strapped to their backs rushed headlong out of the van. A disjointed squad of reporters sprang at us from beneath a copse of shadowy evergreens.

"They're here! They're here," someone called out in French.

There was a loud thump on the car's hood.

A face pressed against my window; it was shaggy-bearded, distorted. Another face peeped into the rear window.

"Why have you come to France? No, no, you are not Kathleen! Where is Kathleen Beavier?"

Lights blazed all around us: camera lights, headlights, security lamps. Over the commotion came the bleating wail of a police siren.

The car lurched forward as our driver stepped hard on the accelerator. A reporter clinging to the hood was flung into the shrubbery.

I peered into the darkness, searching for some unknown enemy, and I fixed on a man standing calmly in the shadows. He had long black hair and wire-rimmed glasses. He was wearing a khaki coat that looked glaringly bright in the headlights.

I watched him flick a cigarette into the road. It made a slow, graceful arc. The icily calm, insolent way he stared at us gave me a knot in my stomach.

Who was he? Why was he there? I didn't like it. I felt in my heart that he shouldn't be here—nor should the reporters. Who had leaked the information?

A minute later, our car pulled up to the front door of the villa and we were being hustled inside.

Strangers took away our coats and led us into a huge parlor, lit by a roaring fire. There we were joined by Charles and Carolyn Beavier, who had arrived before us. I hugged Carolyn, and Charles surprised me by grasping my hand and then pulling me into an embrace.

I guess we were all family now.

A housekeeper brought us tea, and I let Charles pour a drop of whiskey into it. I wanted so desperately to feel safe and warm and unafraid.

It was a lapse in judgment—understandable, but a lapse all the same. I forgot about the darkness and the fog. I forgot about the menace outside.

I thought only about Kathleen and Colleen and their babies.

70

Father Rosetti leaned in close to Kathleen. "Listen to me, child. You *must* pay attention now. Nothing in your life has prepared you for this." He paused and choked out a humorless laugh. "And nothing in my life has prepared *me* for this."

"That's comforting," Kathleen said.

"Well." Rosetti smiled thinly. "While your attitude is understandable, given the natural insolence of your age, it isn't very comforting."

"I'm sorry," Kathleen said. "I don't know where we are, or *why* we're here. Of course I'm a little freaked out."

Rosetti nodded. "I understand. We are here together because it's essential that I spend some time with you."

"You're testing me? Still?"

"I suppose I am. I *will* tell you that we're on our way to Rome."

Kathleen turned and gazed out the window of the second-class train compartment. She was in France now—she thought—but was on her way to Italy. How had this become her life? As the train bore down a blurred tunnel, the overhead lights flickered and died.

Rosetti was still talking. He was trying to communicate an important point, she could tell, but she was so tired. Body and soul.

She felt her homesickness as grief. Where did she belong now? And what of the baby?

"Kathleen, please allow me to tell you one thing," Rosetti was saying. "It's something I believe, something the Church in Rome believes, and something that I will ask you to try to accept on faith also."

She turned toward him and nodded. She had to pay close attention, since his accent made some of the words difficult to follow. But her eyes felt so heavy.

"I believe that evil is a powerful and tangible force on earth. It is as real as you and I are real. The Devil exists, Kathleen, and his ways are unfathomable to us. He is a master of deception. He can seem not to be anywhere, but he is *everywhere*.

"Those who would deny the existence of true evil are denying what they see in the world: what they hear about, what they think about and feel almost every day of their lives. They are denying what they read in newspapers. Evil is all around us right now, Kathleen. I know this to be true."

She wrapped her arms tightly around her chest. "You're scaring me," she said softly, "and I was already so scared. I can't take it. I can't listen anymore."

"You must fear the Devil," Rosetti said, "not a little harmless darkness, not the *words* I'm saying."

The ceiling lights suddenly flickered back on. Kathleen stared into the priest's dark eyes. She did believe him. She'd seen it, smelled it, felt it in the air. She was never far from evil now. Not for a minute. And she felt at the mercy of whatever or whomever laid claim to her.

For the first time in her life, Kathleen believed in the Devil. She knew he was close, maybe right there on the train.

He didn't want her to have this baby.

71

Colleen heard the dogs going wild outside. She put down her history textbook and struggled out of the rocking chair. She'd always gotten straight As and she saw no reason to let her grades slip now.

It took her a moment to get to the front door, but when she did, her mouth dropped open.

A bright orange bus with the words DUBLIN TOURS in fancy script had pulled up on the road right in front of her house.

People, mostly women but a few men and children, were getting off and looking around themselves in amazement.

A blonde in a green coat came forward while the others hung back.

Colleen tentatively stepped onto the stone stoop. "Can I help you?" she called.

The blonde smiled pleasantly. "Please excuse us if we're intruding."

Colleen didn't understand. "I'm sorry—why are you here?"

The woman flushed slightly, looked almost embarrassed. "Oh, dear, dear. We tried to call ahead, but the cell signal out here... well, it simply doesn't exist. But we've traveled all the way from Dublin to see Colleen Galaher."

"You have?" Colleen whispered. Her hand shook on the doorknob.

"Might you be Colleen?" the woman asked, her voice gentle. Hopeful.

Colleen stood straighter. "I am," she said. "And why would you be coming all the way from Dublin to see me?"

Another woman stepped forward from the group clustered by the bus. "My mother and my sister live in the village. They told me about your special situation."

"My name is Sister Eleanor," said the blonde. "And I talked to a friend of mine at your school about—"

"We're here because of the baby," the woman by the bus broke in. "We hear it's miraculous. There was a priest from the Vatican here!"

Colleen didn't know what to do. She couldn't be angry at these nice people from Dublin. And besides, she craved company—and maybe even the attention they were giving her.

"I'd invite you inside, but..." She gestured toward the small house.

Sister Eleanor shook her head. "There's no need of that, child. Just seeing you is enough. This is worth our entire trip. Seeing you, hearing your voice, is our reward."

Suddenly tears came into Colleen's eyes; she started to weep.

Someone believed in her.

Someone finally believed.

72

When I awoke from my deep sleep, I found that I was still so exhausted I could barely move my arms and legs.

I lay in a big, soft bed in a manor in the French countryside. As I pulled the lavender-scented linens up to my chin, I thought about Kathleen and Colleen. I hoped they had gotten through the night all right.

The time was close for both of them, and I wondered if they might deliver their babies on the same day, at the same hour—maybe even at the same moment. It seemed to me that anything could happen now.

God, I thought to myself, *I believe. I really do believe.*

And at that very instant I heard a voice. It wasn't in the room but somewhere inside my head. I recognized it from a long time ago, when I was little. When I believed hard and prayed even harder.

It was the voice I had talked with in my prayers. Sometimes it seemed male and at other times female, but it was always under-standing, kind, loving.

I need your help. I spoke to this presence inside my mind. *Please help all of us on this earth, but especially those two poor girls.*

Then I heard its message: *You must be brave and strong now, Anne. That's why you're here. You are the bravest of all. You've been put here for a purpose.*

I took comfort in those words, even though I didn't really understand what they meant. What was my purpose?

I supposed I would find out. For the first time in so long, I believed, and I loved the feeling.

And, I think, I was loved.

73

Rome.

A burly old man in a beret and a navy greatcoat walked slowly down a cobbled alley off the Viale dell'Università. The Termini, named for the train station nearby, was a seedy maze of streets and alleyways. Feral cats slunk through the shadows, their unblinking eyes watching the stooped old man from underneath parked cars and from perches on the ruins of the Baths of Diocletian.

The stranger stopped in front of one of the looming gray buildings, his eyes roaming up the dirty windows. He saw a bent television antenna on the roof and a peeling billboard for Absolut. He noticed the cats. Then the old man stiffly climbed the crumbling front steps and pulled a dangling bell.

A stout middle-aged woman with a dragging limp finally came to the door. She held a cat in her arms.

"Buon giorno, signora. Per favore, desidero una camera tranquilla." ("Good day, madam. Please, I need a quiet room.")

Signora Ducci quickly took in the large, poorly dressed man.

He was in his late fifties or sixties, she guessed. Still strong-looking. A workman, no doubt. Not likely to die during the winter, at least.

"I have a room—I must have one month in advance." The woman stiffened her lower jaw to show her intransigence on that point. Her cat uttered a soft hiss.

"I only wish to stay a week or two, *signora*."

"One month in advance. That is my rule. There are many other rooms in Rome."

Sighing, the man said, "I will pay what you wish."

An hour later, Signora Ducci saw the man climbing the front stairs with a young girl by his side. The girl wore baggy clothes, but she seemed pretty at a quick glance. She didn't appear to be resisting him.

Signora Ducci smiled. *So he has a child bride,* she thought. She'd seen something strange and fearful in the man's eyes, but now she knew what it was—lust.

Upstairs in the old building, Nicholas Rosetti closed the dirty curtains and then opened his greatcoat.

He locked the door.

He thought that he had found a perfect hideaway for himself and Kathleen. He was here to test her, to investigate—but also to protect the girl.

If he possibly could.

74

Three stories above the dark street, a bright yellow square of light shone brightly, like an oblong star, over the humble Roman district.

Kathleen sat behind the window. Her arms were holding her stomach, and it was almost as if she could feel the baby's heartbeat racing inside her. She hadn't been this frightened since her visit to the abortion clinic. But actually, this was worse.

Anything can happen to me now. People have been shot, people have died. The world's racked with plagues and sickness. It feels like we're in biblical times.

Like the end of the world.

But she tried to put those thoughts out of her mind.

I'm going to be a mother—soon. Nothing matters but my child. I won't let it. I love this baby. My baby will make everything right.

Across the small room cluttered with newspapers and food containers from lunch and dinner, Rosetti prayed in a barely audible whisper. The priest was so intense, so focused on the unseen and unknowable, that he scared her.

She turned to the small TV set balanced on top of a packing crate. A reporter spoke in Italian while video clips showed the ongoing hunt for her through Western Europe. There was a report that she'd been spotted in France, and another that she had gone underground in Texas.

This time last year she'd been playing field hockey, sailing on Easton Bay, crewing for the Newport Newts. Now she sat hunched over her big belly in a small, dingy room in Rome, locked away with no one but an old priest. How had *this* become her life?

"You said to tell you when I was ready, Father," Kathleen finally said in a tremulous voice. "I think I'm ready."

Rosetti snapped to attention. He opened his black satchel and took out several items: a cross, a stole, a silver rosary, a small bottle of holy water, and two thick black books. Shadows seemed to flit in the corners of Kathleen's vision, as if there were someone else— some*thing* else—in the room.

"I'll tell you what's going to happen, Kathleen. First, I will read from this." Rosetti held up a cloth book with a blood-red cross on its cover. "It's called the Roman Ritual. Some of the most powerful prayers ever written are contained in this book."

Kathleen felt herself stiffen. "Is this an *exorcism?*" she asked.

"No. Not an exorcism. But, Kathleen, I do believe that the Devil is nearby. Maybe in this very room. But something is keeping us safe from him."

"So far," Kathleen said.

"Yes. So far. Let's keep it that way. We will defeat Satan. He can be beaten. He is, after all, only a fallen angel."

Rosetti solemnly kissed a violet stole, then dropped it over the slope of his broad shoulders. Kathleen could see that his large hands were shaking.

There was a tremor in his voice, too. "The Evil Presence is sometimes called Moloch. Did you know that, Kathleen? Or Mormo—which means King of the Ghouls. Or Beelzebub—which means Lord of Flies. In parts of Africa people still call him Damballa, the Beast. But in Europe, in America, he no longer has a name. That is because so many Westerners no longer believe in Satan. He seems invisible, but he is *everywhere*."

Rosetti solemnly blessed himself. Then the wide-shouldered man began to sweep across the room toward Kathleen. His eyes never left her face. She wanted to run from him, but she didn't—she couldn't. Her body seemed nailed to the chair.

The trembling girl began praying in a loud voice. "Lord God, my Father, protect the child inside of me. Please protect my baby."

75

Father Rosetti paused, as if he didn't want to begin the holy ritual yet. *Because he knew what to expect.* First, the sense of the dreaded, all-pervasive Presence. Then the chilling, unforgettable *Voice.* Then, perhaps, an appearance by the Evil One himself.

When he had been struck down outside the Vatican gates, he had seen, through his torment, a multitude of devils—and he felt them here, too. They were like a sea of vermin.

He held a silver pocket watch in his hand. His parents had given it to him on the day of his ordination. Now he let Kathleen see the face of the antique watch. "Quarter to twelve," he told her. He took a deep breath.

"Dear Lord, please give us a sign." Rosetti began the most important prayer of his life. He felt such hopelessness in the face of the abyss. He believed with all his heart that he was taking the first step into Hell.

"Which virgin will bear our Holy Savior? Which virgin will bear the hateful Beast of this age?" he asked. His voice was different—it sounded like a stranger's.

"Hateful Beast? What do you mean?" Kathleen asked.

Almost at once, she could feel the dark Presence herself. She saw black shapes, glinting eyes, scales, forked tongues.

"Can you see them, Father?" she whispered, terrified. "Please say you can."

"Leave us now!" he suddenly shouted, and sprinkled holy water at the teeming forms.

At the touch of the water, they shrieked and turned to smoke. But then they became animals—terrible chimera, dogs with horse heads, cats with snake tongues.

"They're devils, aren't they?" she asked. "Are these the fallen angels?"

Rosetti didn't speak—only listened, watched. The beasts circled. They watched Kathleen with hunger. With a terrible *possessiveness*.

They stared at her stomach, never blinking. Would they try to eat the child?

"Can you still see them?" Kathleen asked Rosetti.

"I can see whatever you see, Kathleen. Have you laid eyes on them before?"

"No," she said. "Well, I have seen them in dreams. But they're not real. They can't be."

"What happens in the dreams?" Father Rosetti asked. "You must tell me everything you can. Hold nothing back."

Kathleen trembled. "They surround me. They reach out for me. I try to run but they chase me..."

And sometimes these creatures turn into men, she wanted to say.

They circled slowly around her. Kathleen knew they would devour her if they could. Why didn't they attack? They kept eyeing her stomach—wouldn't look away.

And then—as she'd feared—they became wild-eyed men with hard faces and cruel hands. Reaching for her.

Finally, the leader spoke, and she recognized the Voice that had been inside her head for so many months.

"I only want what is mine, what the Father *promised* to me, cheating, lying bastard that he is. I want the child. My child."

"The men are here," she gasped.

"Who?" Father Rosetti leaned in close.

"The men. The ones who tell me..."

"Who tell you what?" he demanded.

"That I'm not a virgin at all."

"Kathleen," the priest asked, "have you ever *known* a man? Have you known these men?"

At that moment, they all rushed at her. They were growling, moaning, making grotesque animal sounds and a kind of group hissing that sounded like the word *yessss. Yesssss. Yessssss!* She retched. They entered her—everywhere they could.

She felt unspeakable shame and guilt. She didn't want the priest to see this. She knew that they were here to hurt the baby.

"This is our child!" the Voice screamed. "We fucked you and you conceived. Tell the priest! Confess. Tell God! Tell the truth!"

Kathleen screamed, and it was an unearthly sound. Her arms beat the air. Her legs thrashed about furiously. Her head shook back and forth. Her eyes rolled up into her head.

Then they were gone. Just like that.

The room was silent.

Kathleen was blinking her eyes rapidly, not comprehending what had just happened to her.

There was only Rosetti. And his silver pocket watch.

"What happened?" she whispered, looking around the empty room, her eyes wide with terror.

"I hypnotized you," he said. "Perhaps it was all in your mind, Kathleen."

76

Sister Katherine Dominica went to Colleen's house that same night, after the bus from Dublin had departed. The nun sat across from Colleen in the small living room, by the flickering light of the peat fire.

"Your mother? She's sleeping already?" the nun asked.

"She's awake. But you almost wouldn't know it. Most of the time she doesn't even seem to know who I am."

The nun nodded. "That must be very hard for you, Colleen."

"We get along fine," the girl said. "We make do."

"We haven't heard any more from that priest from Rome, have we?"

Colleen couldn't help frowning. "I haven't. Have you?"

"Mmm," the old nun said. "There was a bus in town today. Do you know anything about it?"

So *that* was it. Now Colleen understood why the nun had come to visit. She wanted to say that she had no idea what Sister

Katherine was talking about, but she couldn't lie. Not even to the nosy old nun.

"The bus stopped here," she admitted. "There were nuns on board, and lay brothers, too. They came to see me, Sister, because they heard about my...special situation."

The nun clucked her tongue softly. "Was that all?"

Colleen thought about her answer. "They said—that they believed the Savior would be born in Ireland. Isn't that a wonderful thing? They believe in a virgin birth, Sister. In miracles. Do you?"

77

I heard a loud *gong* as the clock struck midnight. It was two days before the babies were due to be born.

Kathleen's.

Colleen's.

Justin and I hadn't left the villa since breakfast, seventeen hours ago. We'd spent all day combing the internet for news of Kathleen and her whereabouts. There were a million theories, but nothing had been confirmed. The Vatican had refused to issue a statement. And they wouldn't put us in touch with Father Rosetti or Kathleen.

Justin shut his laptop with a snap. "This is crazy, Anne. Are we expected to just sit here and wait for the birth—the births? Was there *anything* that Father Rosetti might have said? Anything Kathleen said at any time? Where in hell could they be?"

I shook my head. I had no idea.

He ran his hand through his thick black hair and sighed.

I wished I could comfort him.

Comfort myself.

When I wasn't thinking of the babies, or of all the world's horrors, I was thinking about being here with Justin. I couldn't help it. There had to be a reason for it. There was a plan, I was sure of it. We just didn't know what it was.

"I'm going for a walk. I need some air," I said. "Want to come?"

"Yeah," he said. "I do."

In the last hour the fog had turned into a soft dense sheet of rain. Outside the walled compound, speeding cars hissed by and TV vans idled near the gates. The reporters were as mystified as we were by Kathleen's disappearance, but they weren't about to pull up their stakes here.

Justin opened a big umbrella, and we stepped out onto a gravel path winding between topiary shrubs and dormant rosebushes. The night air smelled sweet and clean and our footsteps crunched in unison.

But I couldn't make myself relax. I hadn't been completely honest with Justin, and that thought was making me sad. I didn't know how much longer we had together.

I had guarded myself from feelings of affection and love for so long, but now they engulfed me. *Why now?*

I had to say something to him. I had to tell the truth.

"I can't stop thinking about you." I said it quickly before I lost my nerve. They were probably the bravest words I'd ever said in my life.

Justin's footsteps slowed, but I pressed his arm and propelled him forward.

"I've been protecting myself from you ever since the day I met you. But it hasn't done much good, has it? My life lately seems to be a blur of strange, nerve-racking moments, with you in the middle of them." I laughed at myself; I couldn't help it.

Justin smiled, too.

"It isn't funny," I said. But I was still laughing.

The two of us walked on, arm in arm. I liked the feeling.
Really liked it.

The path led to a beautiful kitchen garden. Espaliered fruit trees hugged the walls. Rows of winter crops—including kale, leeks, Brussels sprouts—sprang up in neat rows. It looked like a tapestry of the Garden of Eden.

Rain dripped from the rib tips of the umbrella onto my shoes. I looked up, directly into Justin's face. His eyes were so beautiful, so honest and fine, that I swear I felt I could see into his soul.

My voice quavered when I spoke. "Next week we'll most likely be apart again. And I just want to tell you—I *need* to tell you—that I do love you. More than I ever imagined was possible. I don't know why I'm saying—"

His kiss was so gentle I wanted to cry. I lingered over the feel of his lips, trying to memorize every sensation. I was using the kiss to convey the strength of my feelings, to apologize for all the times I'd rebuffed him, and to learn what it felt like to embrace another person with my whole heart.

I felt the umbrella fall to the ground. Heard it blow down the rocky path.

Justin swept me up in his powerful arms and we kissed again. This time it was a more demanding kiss. It asked for surrender, and I was ready to give it. Nothing had ever made me feel this wonderful, this alive. For a long, long time I had wanted someone to love me like this. I realized suddenly why it had never happened. I'd been unable to give love back—but now I could.

Justin pulled away, breathing hard, and I opened my eyes. It was then that I saw someone watching us.

What the hell? I thought. *Who's there?*

Then I realized who it was: the dark-haired man in the khaki raincoat from the night before—the one who'd frightened me when we were just arriving.

"Justin, someone's there. He's behind you. I saw him last night, too."

Justin turned and called out in a sharp voice, "What are you doing here? Hey, *you!*"

The man started to back away, but we wouldn't let him go so easily. I guess we were hungry for answers—any answers at all.

Justin and I started to run. We chased the man back into the groves of apple trees directly behind the garden house. We were gaining on him. We were going to get our answer after all.

The man realized it, too, because he stopped moving away. He stood there and waited for us. He watched us coming through the rain, and then he began to laugh contemptuously.

"You *know* me," he finally said when we were only yards away. "You know exactly who I am. I am your desires."

And then, right before our eyes, he was no longer there.

He had *vanished*.

"Did you see that?" I asked Justin.

"We both did! He was right there."

A voice called out as we stood staring in disbelief at the spot where the man had been.

"Justin, Anne! Are you out there? Anne? Where are you?"

It was Carolyn Beavier. She had a flashlight and a cell phone clutched in her hands.

"It's Kathleen," she cried. "God, it's Kathleen calling. She's safe."

I rushed over to her, taking the telephone and pressing it to my ear. I strained to hear her words.

"Anne—will you please come get me? Will you come *now?*" Kathleen sobbed. "I'm ready to have my baby."

78

Justin and I flew to Rome the following morning to meet Kathleen and Father Rosetti. We were so close to the births now that I was anxious all the time. And Rosetti's mysterious games didn't help things.

The Italian national police and soldiers from the Italian army had succeeded in diverting the paparazzi away from our arrival gate. We found a queue of chunky little Fiat taxis, and parked on the other side of them was our limousine.

I held Justin's hand as the limo sped along the rain-slicked Via Cristoforo Colombo, then into the center of Rome. The driver plunged us into the shadows of the ancient buildings of the Termini.

"Why are they staying here and not at the Vatican?" I wondered out loud. "What is Rosetti *thinking?*"

Justin's eyes surveyed the cold gray city streets. "I keep thinking of the battle between the Archangel Michael and Lucifer with his legions—an epic battle between good and evil."

"We need Michael and *all* his angels," I said, only half-kidding. "Doesn't it seem like the powers of darkness are winning?"

"Maybe," Justin said grimly.

Our car braked at the curb of a particularly disreputable-looking street in the Termini. We got out and hurriedly climbed the steep front steps of a crumbling old building.

The front door was unlocked. Inside, stairs climbed darkly upward.

We quickly mounted splintered flights to a top-floor hallway. Before us were three dirty gray doors and a wired-over skylight, dim with soot. A black cat shot out of a corner and scared both of us.

Justin turned to me. "It gets stranger and stranger."

"This is the part where the movie audience always screams, 'Don't go in there!' "

"So of course we do," he said. And then he smiled, and the hallway almost seemed to brighten a little.

One of the doors opened suddenly, and my heart jumped. Nicholas Rosetti stood in the frame, backlit by lamplight that flooded the hall and stairs.

"Justin and Anne, thank God. Please, come in. Thank you for coming."

Rosetti attempted a smile, but his face was haggard and drained. He must have dropped twenty pounds since I saw him less than a week ago. The skin on his face was sallow and papery. The Vatican investigator looked as if he was dying before our eyes.

"Are you all right?" I asked him.

"Of course, of course." He patted my shoulder and led the way inside. "I'm tougher than I look, and I look tough."

Across the small, bare room, Kathleen was propped up on a beat-up sofa. She pushed herself up and waddled awkwardly to us. She also looked ashen and exhausted.

She got her arms around me and began to cry. "I'm so glad to see you," she sobbed. "I'm so afraid. This is so awful. Being pregnant, being *here*. We have to talk, Anne."

Something in her voice chilled me. "What's going on?" I turned and glared at Rosetti. "What have you done to her? Why are you here? Kathleen needs to be around doctors."

He waved away my concern as if it were too trivial to respond to. "I simply don't have time to explain everything to you!" He spoke to me in a sharp tone that matched mine. "Kathleen would have been unsafe anywhere except with me. If you don't understand that, so be it. And now I have to move her again. The baby must be born at the pope's own hospital. The Salvator Mundi."

79

Justin was tall and strongly built, and he moved toward Rosetti like fury made flesh. "You risked *her life*—and the child's," he shouted.

Rosetti stood his ground. "I did no such thing. I would never put a life in jeopardy. You just don't understand the facts of the situation."

"Tell us something *factual,* then," Justin shouted, the veins bulging out in his neck. He still looked ready to punch out Father Rosetti. "What do you know? *Tell us!*"

I put my hand on Justin's arm, felt his tension and strength. "Father Rosetti, we're sick of being in the dark," I said. "You say you need help, but you never give us a reason. *Believe,* you say. Believe what?"

Rosetti's posture slumped. "I'm sorry," he said, his voice ragged with fatigue. "I do trust both of you. It is a very difficult thing for me, but I do. I know how you care for Kathleen. I know you are both good. That's why you're here. But I can't. I promised. Oh, God..."

And then he began to speak of an intensely frightened pope who knew a terrifying secret. "And then," said Rosetti, "the pope was struck dead in his sleep! I had already accepted my mission. Before then, I was an ordinary priest in the Congregation of Sacred Rites. My qualifications for the job were that I was a thorough investigator and a good priest. I am a detective for the Church.

"*If* you help me now," Father Rosetti went on, "you will know everything soon. Every last twist and infernal turn and trick of the abominable Beast! Are you sure you want to know what I must do? Are you prepared to confront the Evil One? Are you both in a state of grace?"

"Are *you?*" I challenged Rosetti. "You look like a madman. You expect us to do as you say because you come from the high-and-mighty Vatican, the Holy See. Tell us the truth. *Tell us now!*"

Rosetti sighed, shook his head, and then gave in, or at least seemed to. He whispered so that only we could hear.

"The Devil is to be born as a human child very soon. Only then can the legions multiply and take over the earth. But a savior is to be born as well. A savior will be born to one of the two virgins. Anne, Justin, I still don't know which girl it is. You must help me find out."

80

Early the following morning, we waited for Kathleen and Rosetti in a small, dreary café in the Termini. I was so jumpy I couldn't sit still, and the double espresso I'd just drunk wasn't helping.

Did I really want to know what Rosetti claimed to know? Did I want to play by his rules?

Was I prepared to confront evil, whatever that might turn out to be?

The questions seemed absurd, the stuff of movies and melodrama. But I had to know the answers. And I really did believe that something monumental was going to happen—I just didn't know what.

Our tiny metal table was jammed in between a radiator, a pistachio-green wall hung with music scores, and a large man feeding tidbits to his schnauzer. It was hard to talk over the breakfast-hour din, but in a way the noise and the smells were reassuring. It seemed *normal*. The real world still existed.

We'd spent the night on the floor of the room Rosetti had rented for himself and Kathleen. He had been in constant prayer throughout the night, his features contorted as if he was in terrible pain.

In the gloom, illuminated only by the faint glow of a street-light, I imagined that Rosetti was standing watch. A lone sentry listening for the approach of... *what?* Another plague? Demons? His own death?

And then he talked to us, and it took him the better part of an hour. He told us what we had to do and why. He said we had two choices: We could walk away, or we could take our chances that he was right.

Justin looked into my eyes. "We don't have to do what Rosetti has asked of us, Anne."

I knew Justin was questioning his faith, but perversely, mine had solidified. "Justin, I do. Rosetti *is* from the Congregation of Sacred Rites. He's for real. And so are Kathleen and Colleen. We have to help him."

Justin nodded. We were upset and scared and exhausted. We were also going to be separated in a few minutes. One of us was to go with Kathleen to Vatican City. The other had to go to Ireland, to be with Colleen. One of us might be in terrible danger. Maybe both of us.

As Rosetti had warned us, this wasn't about everyday, run-of-the-mill pain and suffering—it was about eternal pain and suffering.

Without being aware, I'd crumbled my *papassino* to powder. Justin pushed his plate aside and dropped some coins onto the table. We stood and awkwardly negotiated our way out of the café and onto the street.

I stopped just beyond the doorway and reached out for him. I pressed my face into his sweater and felt his arms come around me.

Tears flowed down my cheeks and I didn't even try to stop them. I'd changed so much recently that I hardly knew who I was anymore. Once I'd finally allowed myself to feel, I couldn't contain my emotions. Feelings rushed through me in great, dizzying waves.

"I love you," I sobbed into Justin's chest. "Why couldn't I have told you such a simple thing?"

"Maybe because it isn't so simple," he answered.

He held me tightly, resting his cheek on the top of my head, swaying with me gently while Italian pedestrians parted around us. He was so strong, so good. How had I ever given him up? What was going to happen to us now?

"I'll be back," he said. "I promise."

Two dark-blue sedans arrived at the curb outside the dismal building where we'd spent the past twenty-four hours. Kathleen and Rosetti finally appeared. I stared at her face. She still looked pale and stricken. She would go into labor soon.

Then what?

Last night she'd fallen asleep so quickly and slept so soundly that we'd never had a chance to talk. Then this morning, it almost seemed that Rosetti was keeping Kathleen away from me.

It was time to go, time for Justin and me to part.

I would go with Kathleen.

And Justin would go with Rosetti to Colleen.

We hugged one final time, and I was struck with the awful thought that I would never see Justin O'Carroll again.

81

As Justin waited in the sedan, Father Rosetti took both my hands in his. The touch was surprisingly gentle. He seemed almost human again.

He whispered, "Anne, what I'm about to ask will horrify you. It will go against everything you stand for. But I have to get your promise."

My mouth was dry as I listened. I prayed for strength. I had no idea where he was going with this, but I believed him when he said I'd hate it.

Rosetti continued. "I hope that I'll soon know the final truth about the two young virgins. The message of Fátima has provided a trail to be followed. The Bible has provided clues in the apocalyptic writings." Rosetti's eyes scrunched up as if he'd suddenly received a blow. "But, Anne, I'm not certain. Ultimately, this will be a matter of faith. It will not be simple. Nothing ever is."

"*Tell* me about it," I said under my breath.

Rosetti's voice intensified. "You must watch for a clear sign. A sign at the moment of the birth was promised. We will know which child is the Beast and which is the Savior. *You* will know."

I felt as if I were watching myself in a dream; everything was unreal and nothing made any sense.

"But then what do I do?" I begged.

He was resolute. "Anne, the Beast must be killed. The child of the Devil must be destroyed. And the child of God must be protected at any cost to us. *Any* cost."

Reading my shock, Rosetti made the sign of the cross. "You will know what to do when the time comes," he whispered. "That's why you're here."

I stumbled then, and Rosetti gripped my shoulders. Made me look him in the eye. I had faith, yes. But trusting in God was one thing, and killing a newborn infant was another. Could I do it? I didn't think I could ever kill again.

"I d-don't know, Father," I stammered.

"I believe in you, Anne," Rosetti said. "You are a good person. You are the strongest of all of us. You can defeat the Beast."

82

Was that why I was going with Kathleen? Because I was supposedly a strong person? And why were both Justin and Rosetti going to Ireland? Why had the attention shifted to Colleen?

I entered the cool interior of the waiting car. Kathleen reached for me and I hugged her, feeling sick at heart. Would I have to betray her and her child? Would I have to do much worse than that?

Two Swiss Guards sat in the front of the Vatican vehicle—a driver, and... what? A guard? It made me wonder about Rosetti and Kathleen's escapades the past few days, but as I had always known, the Church works in strange and mysterious ways.

As we pulled away from the curb, I was startled by a swarm of police on motorcycles. They appeared suddenly and flanked our car. I looked at Kathleen in confusion, but a moment later, I understood why the extra security was needed. Kathleen's whereabouts had apparently gotten out.

The sidewalks were a solid mass of pushing, screaming people—

all trying to get a look at the young American virgin. Thousands of them—the faithful, the curious, and the skeptical—were packed on both sides of the narrow roadways and even hanging off the heavy stone overpasses.

Kathleen gripped my arm so tightly she nearly cut off the circulation. I could hardly breathe as we approached the gates of the Vatican.

"My God, Kathleen," I whispered. "This is all for you."

"No, Anne," she said. "It's not for me at all. None of it is. It's for him. It's for the child inside me."

We cast glances at the great Vatican towers, the stucco palaces, and the gold crosses blazing against the vast blue skies. Banked deep in front of the small shops and trattorias on the Via Merulana, a two-mile-long column of worshippers greeted the virgin.

Our driver spoke in broken English. "They saying two hundred thousand people, and it just starting."

Flowers bombarded the car as we drove past the huge crowd, and the sealed windows couldn't drown out all those shouts of joy.

The part of me that was still a good Christian understood completely. These people wanted desperately to believe in something. And the magnitude of the crowd, the devotion and the honest love in the eyes of the people—it humbled me. And it gave me chills to think what effect a miracle would have in this supposedly rational, scientific age. My skin tingled all over and I felt light-headed.

As I entered the Vatican for the first time in my life, sitting with a young girl who supposedly would give birth to the Messiah, I felt my doubt fly away on great white wings.

I believed once again, and it was the best feeling I could imagine.

83

I turned to Kathleen and took her hand. "You wanted to talk," I said.

"I do," she said. "I remembered something when I was with Father Rosetti these past few days. Wait until we're in the hospital and settled in. I'll tell you then. There's time."

"Is there?" I asked. "Are you sure?"

"Yes, I am." Her eyes turned back to the street. "My God, look at all of those people."

Kathleen had no idea why she'd been chosen for this, but she did know one thing: She knew her purpose. She knew why she'd been put on Earth. I couldn't imagine ever having such certainty, and certainly not at seventeen.

When the car came to a stop outside the hospital where she would deliver, I saw a colorful wall of the Swiss Guard awaiting our arrival. They quickly drew a protective circle around the car, holding back the mob of people waving handkerchiefs and jumping and bobbing to get a glimpse of Kathleen.

Rows of priests in white surplices and flowing black cassocks knelt and crossed themselves. They seemed swept up in ecstasy. I felt their love as a physical force, and it was overwhelming.

I got out of the car and gave Kathleen a hand. As she climbed out and touched her feet to the ground, a loud, thunderous roar swept up the avenue.

Tears suddenly slipped down Kathleen's cheeks. I didn't cry, but I was close. I remembered Rosetti's words: *You are the strongest of all of us.* Why did I need to be strong?

My eyes drifted over the surging, brightly colored mass. I saw a crack in the wall of guards and police. A quick movement.

Then I saw him! My heart leapt in my throat.

It was the watcher.

Over the din, I shouted as loud as I could, "Over there! Stop him!"

I was pointing to a man in a khaki-colored raincoat, with slick black hair and wire-rimmed glasses. He was the man from the French countryside—the one who had disappeared before my eyes. The Devil? One of the fallen angels? An assassin?

He was pushing through the opening, moving swiftly toward Kathleen. Something in his hand sparkled in the sunlight.

"Gun!" I shouted. "Gun!"

But I didn't have mine—it was packed away. The man was bent low. Coming even faster now. Then he was running toward us with his right arm extended.

"He has a gun!" I screamed again.

Then I hurled myself between the onrushing man and Kathleen. I didn't even give it a thought.

Sound stopped and time elongated. My neck twisted sharply to the right. My chest bucked as it received a terrific jolting blow.

I felt the crush of falling soldiers and police. It was as if I had been sucked into a deep, dark hole.

There was a bright white explosion at the center of the thick wall of people. Kathleen screamed high and long. I screamed, too.

The pile of frightened policemen thrashed wildly, their batons rising and falling.

I could hear Kathleen, but I couldn't see her. "Anne," she wailed. "Anne!"

I was lying on the ground. I could see the man in the raincoat, bleeding from head and neck wounds. As he was dragged toward a police van, he pinned me with his eyes. He spoke in English, his mouth spewing hatred.

"Kathleen Beavier is not of God! You must destroy her. *You* must destroy the child. *You* must do it."

Suddenly I wasn't sure if he was the same man we'd seen in France. My vision blurred and spun. Everything was happening so quickly. I forced myself to my feet against the urging of Italian policemen.

"Kathleen!" I shouted as I saw her being taken into the hospital.

She stopped and waited for me. Then the two of us hurried inside the heavy doors. We hugged each other tightly.

"I thought you were dead. Shot," she sobbed. *So did I.* "Oh, Anne, I was so afraid for you."

"I'm fine, I'm just fine," I murmured as we held on tight. Somehow, I was fine.

This is a good girl, I kept thinking. The Devil couldn't be inside this young woman. Not inside Kathleen. Colleen Galaher had to be the one.

And yet she had seemed such a good girl, too.

BOOK 3
NATIVITY

84

Colleen felt surprisingly good, considering how close she was to term. *I'm going to be a real mother soon! A wee tiny baby is going to come out of me,* she thought. It was still astonishing to her. It brought a happiness that kept her going most days, and then through the long nights at the cottage.

She was making afternoon tea for herself, her mother, and Sister Katherine. She cut into a dark loaf of soda bread marked with the traditional cross.

The simple act of tea-making kept her mind off everything happening now, the things that didn't make any sense to her and the things that possibly never would.

How will I take care of my mother and the little one? Will I be able to go back to school?

"I'm only sixteen years old," the young girl finally whispered. Her small, freckled hands trembled so hard that the lid rattled on the teapot. "Somebody please help me."

Colleen brought the steaming tea and still-warm bread out into the tiny living room. Where was Sister Katherine? She had been sitting there only moments before.

Colleen called her name. No answer. Her mother had fallen asleep again, and she wouldn't wake for hours. Colleen unlatched the front door and went outside.

Sister Katherine was nowhere to be found.

But a dark shape was making its way up the path. Colleen could see it was a priest. *Oh, God, it was Father Flannery from town. How dare he come?*

Colleen crouched behind a clump of gorse, its wiry branches forming a thick barricade. Had he seen her? She thought not.

She couldn't bear to be anywhere near him. There was something wrong with the parish priest—why else would he have kissed her in the rectory?

Colleen walked as quickly as she could to the barn. She pressed her weight against the sliding door. Panting heavily, she slipped inside. She felt tired and breathless. And so terribly alone and afraid.

She heard the pathetic priest calling to her: "Colleen, I've come to bless you, child."

His words made her skin crawl. "God help me, you won't," she whispered.

She cast her eyes around in the gloom of the barn. The straw on the floor seemed to eddy around her feet, and a warm draft brushed her cheek. Grey Lady whickered a greeting. Colleen felt protected by something unseen, something or someone who loved her.

There was a stall at the very back of the barn. It was dark and pungent with the scent of lanolin, occupied now by an old, lonely ewe.

"Hush, Biddy," Colleen spoke to the sheep, pushing her aside. Then she squirreled herself into the farthest corner and covered herself with hay. The smell of it was thick in her nostrils and she nearly sneezed.

Outside, Father Flannery's voice became a plea, a whine. *"Col leen. Come to me, now. I am your priest."*

When he spoke again, his voice was sharp with anger. "Come out, Colleen. I'm here on God's business."

I don't believe it. God doesn't want his servants to molest young girls. God isn't sick—the way you are!

Colleen shut her eyes as tight as she could. Eventually, the only sounds she heard were those of the animals, stamping and chewing in the barn. It was fragrant and peaceful here. A stream of sunshine came through the hayloft, a long, bright shaft of light like a ladder to heaven.

It dawned on her then. It was so fitting; it was perfect. This was where she would give birth to the child.

As it had been in Bethlehem, God had led her to a manger.

85

Nicholas Rosetti had arrived in Maam Cross, and still the dreaded, damnable Voice was with him, trying to distract him from the end of his mission, trying to drive him insane. He was here ahead of Justin O'Carroll, who'd gone to Dublin to meet with a doctor who had examined Colleen.

No one has the right to ask this of you. You will damn yourself to an eternity in Hell, the Voice said into his ear. *Eternity is a long, long time, Nicholas. You have no idea, but I do!*

Father Rosetti struggled into the small hotel room. He dropped his bag onto the thinly carpeted floor. He didn't bother to switch on the overhead lights.

Yes, get used to the dark. You see, there are dark fires in Hell. You didn't know that, did you? But I do.

He walked over to the water-streaked window and stood there, observing the damp, silent Irish village. He had to be close to the truth about the two virgins. And yet he feared that he was committing the sin of pride to believe so.

His night sweats were with him during the day now. His big heart seemed to seize up without warning and dance erratic cadences in his chest. But his mind was still sharp. The Beast had made use of artifice, illusion, imitation, disruption, and misdirection. Nicholas Rosetti could see through it—or at least he thought he could.

He was still alive, wasn't he? He hadn't been condemned to Hell yet.

Soon, Nicholas, the Voice taunted. *You're so very close to the eternal gates of doom. Be careful where you step. Careful, Nick. It's a long, long drop.*

In his satchel were the documents revealing what he knew. Before he left to see Colleen Galaher, the papers would go into the hotel safe.

No place is safe from me, Nicholas. Don't you know that yet?

A rapping sound shattered his troubled reverie. A knock at the door. It should be Justin, thank God.

But it wasn't Justin O'Carroll standing in the hallway. It was a stranger, a man not much more than five and a half feet in height, wearing a coat of good-quality tweed.

He took off his cap, which was wet with rain. "I'm Dennis Murphy. Darcy downstairs said you had arrived," said the man at the door. "*Dr.* Dennis Murphy," he added. "Sixteen years ago I brought little Colleen Galaher into the world. I've been thinking you should see this." He spoke in a heavy brogue.

Rosetti stood mute in the doorway as Dr. Murphy shoved forward an aged manila envelope. It was marked in the upper-right-hand corner with a name, written in pencil, in the careful script born of a Catholic-school education.

Rosetti took the envelope and read the name written on it. *Colleen Galaher.*

Then he ripped open the envelope and read what was inside.

A great ringing sounded in his ears and there was a suffocating constriction in his chest. His vision narrowed and his skin became as cold as ice. This was what he needed to know, wasn't it? This was the sign he'd been searching for. This *had* to be the sign.

He looked up, but Dr. Murphy was no longer there. Rosetti ran out into the hall, but there was no one there, either. He phoned downstairs, and there *was* a Darcy at the front desk.

"Father, I don't understand," she said. "Dennis Murphy? It couldn't be. Dennis Murphy died at least ten years ago."

Rosetti hung up the phone and heard a roar of laughter in his ears.

So where is your precious sign, Nicholas? How will you know the truth? The answer is so simple—you won't.

86

That night, armed guards stood outside Kathleen's door. They watched the hallway, while I scrutinized everyone who came into the room.

There were a lot of strange new faces at the hospital, and as far as I was concerned, every stranger was a possible threat to the baby.

There were supposedly legions of devils, so why couldn't they simply overtake us? What was holding the Evil One at bay? There had to be an explanation for their absence.

I sat on a hard-backed chair beside Kathleen's bed and we watched the news. The assassination attempt led off the newscast. A grim-faced reporter said that Kathleen Beavier had entered Salvator Mundi International Hospital, the private facility where cardinals and even the pope went for the best medical care in Italy. A team of Italian and American doctors would be assisting the birth, which could come at any moment.

The first official report out of Salvator Mundi came from the

Italian chief surgeon himself. We watched the announcement on CNN.

Dr. Leonardo Annunziata was an elegant, dark-haired man in his early forties. "Signorina Kathleen Beavier is in excellent condition," he said smoothly, with only a trace of an accent. "The birth of the child can be anticipated in the next twelve to twenty-four hours. We are expecting no complications whatsoever."

Kathleen and I looked at each other—and we laughed for the first time in days.

"Dr. Annunziata could be in for a surprise," she said.

The news was all bad that night. The natural disasters around the globe continued and actually seemed to be getting worse.

Kathleen and I held hands as we watched. There was no way to connect the plagues and famines to events occurring in Rome and Maam Cross, Ireland, but all my instincts told me that there had to be a link, and that we would soon know what it was.

"Maybe the world is going to end," Kathleen mused. "Or maybe my baby can stop it."

Or make it even worse, I couldn't help thinking.

87

Each hour seemed to take our paranoia to new heights. Time felt too fast and too slow at the same time. The excruciating wait was almost over—but I was still unprepared for the unknown.

Kathleen had at last nodded off, and I needed to take a break to clear my head if I could. I could hardly be her Rock of Gibraltar when I was feeling so wobbly myself.

Take a little walk, I heard. *You deserve it.*

Had I said that? I must have.

I told the guard outside the door that I'd be back in a few minutes. Then I walked down the deserted marble-and-stone hallway, which smelled strongly of disinfectant. Standing within a neat line of religious statues, a young Italian policeman watched me approach, a rifle cradled in his arms like a baby.

"Signorina," he said. He bowed his head, knowing that I was the virgin's companion. "Is she all right? The young girl, Caterina?"

"Yes, everything's fine," I reassured him. "She's sleeping right now."

My shoes squeaked on the spotless floor as I walked, echoing loudly in the early-morning silence. I wondered what Justin and Rosetti were doing. They would probably be at Colleen Galaher's cottage by now.

I thought of Colleen a lot, and always with affection. She was younger than Kathleen and, if anything, even more innocent. I remembered her nearly transparent white skin and the rosy aura that seemed to emanate from her.

Both girls seemed so perfect for the saintly role that only one was destined to play. The other was carrying a monster.

Which girl was which?

And, more agonizingly, if Kathleen was the latter... could I do as Rosetti asked?

Turning another dark stone corner, I found that I'd reached the far end of the hospital building. I'd gone too far.

Struck with sudden anxiety, I turned and practically ran back to the room where Kathleen was sleeping. Was she safe? How could I have been gone so long? What was I thinking?

I burst into the small room. Kathleen was resting peacefully. Breathless, I stared down at her, then watched her sleep gently for a good long time.

Inside Kathleen, I thought, was a baby, upside down in a warm bath of amniotic fluid, cramped now in the place that had housed it for nine months. The head would be close against her cervix. The limbs, fingers, toes, nails, eyebrows, and eyelashes were all fully developed. The heartbeat was steady and fine. The senses of sight, hearing, and touch weren't fully developed but were ready to blossom quickly once exposed to stimuli.

The baby was probably around twenty inches long, a little over seven pounds—quite average in that way. In each tiny brain cell there was all the love and goodness, the capacity for happiness and sadness, the genius, the wit, the love of beauty, and the will for survival within the human race.

In all of those ways, this was a child like any other.

I prayed that Kathleen's baby had drawn the lucky straw, because I doubted with my whole heart that even if it emerged with horns and a tail I'd be strong enough to take away its precious breath.

How could I kill an infant? Any infant? How could anyone do such a thing? But especially, how could *I*?

I sat in my chair, tipped it slightly back. I gazed out through the window in Kathleen's room and watched a burnt-orange and crimson sun rising over Trastevere.

It was a beautiful sunrise.

It was surely a sign.

88

I must have dozed in my chair near her bed. Kathleen groaned loudly in pain, waking me instantly.

"It's time, Anne," she whispered urgently.

It was after six in the morning. We were alone in a large suite at Salvator Mundi, both of us terrified and pretending to each other that we believed all the assurances that we had nothing to worry about.

The hospital building was four stories high, plain straw-colored brick with large, churchlike windows. It was enclosed by a high brick wall and shaded by tall umbrella pines.

I'd heard that outside that wall, eighty thousand people had gathered. Hundreds of thousands more were said to be collecting in St. Peter's Square.

I couldn't help wondering what was happening in tiny Maam Cross, Ireland.

Beside me, in the soothing, pale-blue hospital suite, Kathleen grabbed her belly. She let out a sound that was a cross between a shriek and a moan. Then she relaxed again.

"You're doing great, Kathleen," I said. "Just rest when it doesn't hurt." I felt like this was my birth, too, somehow. "That's it, breathe... and now, rest."

"God, it really hurts," Kathleen gasped. Her face was pale from fatigue and pain. We both knew she wasn't ready to give birth yet. But she was getting closer.

As I placed a damp cloth on her brow, I noticed that she was looking past me. I followed her gaze and saw that we were no longer alone. It scared the hell out of me.

A man was standing in the stone archway leading into the hospital room. A solemn, elderly man whom I recognized immediately.

Pope Clement XVI himself had come to see Kathleen.

The slanting rays of morning sunlight streaming through the window engulfed his narrow shoulders, making him seem as if he were an icon of pure gold. Not like a man at all.

We all stared at one another. Finally, he spoke. "Have you anything to say, Kathleen? Anything to confess?" His voice was forceful. "I'm here to help you."

Kathleen paled.

Then she was struck as if by a fierce seizure. Her eyes rolled back. Her nostrils flared. She opened her mouth wider than I would have thought possible. She began to scream and scream. I'd never been more shocked or scared at any time in my life.

Suddenly, I had the feeling that I didn't know Kathleen at all.

When I looked back to the doorway, I saw that Pope Clement was walking away. He never looked back.

89

A young and handsome dark-haired priest stood lookout on the grand stone terrazza of the Apostolic Palace. More than four hundred thousand people were spread out before him, completely blanketing the majestic piazza of St. Peter's Square, stretching as far as his eyes could see.

He leaned into a microphone and spoke. *Hail Mary, full of Grace.* His rich baritone boomed out over the great sea of heads. *This* was why he had entered the priesthood—this glorious power, this majesty.

The crowd in Rome answered his prayer in a thunderous roar.

In Mexico City, almost a million of the faithful attended an emotional Mass in and around the Basilica of Guadalupe, the site where the Blessed Virgin had appeared to a local Indian in the sixteenth century.

All through Spain and Holland, throughout France and Belgium, in Poland, in Germany, Ireland, and England, the great old cathedrals were filled to capacity once again. The people of Europe wanted something to believe in. Now they had it.

In the United States, too, the churches overflowed. People stuck at work stayed glued to their laptops, their smartphones.

At St. Peter's Square, the young priest's voice continued to echo along the towering, ancient colonnades. "Pray for us sinners, now and at the hour of our death. Amen."

"We trust in the will of God!" The people cried together in a deafening chorus.

All over the world, after all the years of difficulty and decades of apostasy, so many people still believed or came to believe again.

But the plagues and the famines continued unabated. Everywhere, people talked of the end of the world.

Church might be the only refuge left.

90

J ustin and Rosetti had almost reached the Galaher house, and neither of them had ever seen so many birds. The woods were filled with them, and so was the darkening sky.

As the English Ford hummed along the undulating country roads, Justin felt the weight of the heavy metallic sky looming overhead. He was being tested now. There was a powerful voice in his head.

You know you shouldn't be here. Your faith isn't strong enough. You don't even want to be a priest anymore.

You want to be with her. It's the only thing that matters to you now. You love Anne Fitzgerald more than you love God. Leave this place.

Go to Anne.

Or risk something happening to you.

Or her.

He couldn't stop the troubling thoughts—they seemed to be

coming from outside him. He wondered if Father Rosetti sensed his torment, but the priest was stony-faced and silent. When they pulled up to the Galaher house outside Maám Cross, Justin felt a deeper chill in the air. *How strange,* he thought, staring at the unfamiliar stucco bungalow and barn through the dusty windshield.

It isn't as it was before. Something has changed.

"Something's wrong," he muttered as he stopped the sedan in front of the house.

Rosetti still said nothing.

Justin studied the small house. There was an unremembered television antenna, which hung broken, like a snarled branch, off the thatched roof. The grass was pale now, no longer a lush loden green. The house seemed to be listing to one side.

He was almost certain his memory wasn't playing tricks. That everything looked different. But if it wasn't in his mind...

Tricks! he thought. *The Devil plays tricks. Is the Devil here in Maám Cross?*

As they approached, Rosetti grew extremely agitated. He threw open the door without knocking. He searched the house in seconds and then burst back out. His eyes were wide with fear.

"The girl's mother is dead, Justin. She's hanging from the ceiling upstairs. So is the nun from the convent school! We have to find Colleen. Help me."

Dread pounded in Justin's chest as they ran toward the barn. A young priest appeared out of nowhere, a mop of dark hair blowing around his face. He blocked the entrance to the barn. His fists were clenched; his eyes were cold.

"Colleen is in here," said the priest forcefully. "I'm Father Flannery from the parish. I'm taking care of her now. We care for our own."

"Be gone, Satan!" Rosetti bellowed at the priest. "You have no power over me! You have no power over Father O'Carroll. You have no power here on earth! Not yet, anyway."

Rosetti shoved the priest aside with a powerful motion of his arm, but Flannery quickly regained his balance. He rushed at Rosetti and again threw himself between the priest and the doorway.

"You can't go in! This doesn't concern you! This girl is one of ours!"

"No!" Rosetti screamed at the top of his voice. "Never! You have no power over this innocent girl."

As Justin watched, too stunned to move, Rosetti grabbed a pitchfork that was leaning against the barn. *"Get out of my way,"* he warned, his voice thrumming with danger. "Stand aside or I will pierce your infernal heart."

"It's my child," the priest suddenly hissed, his face twisting with rage. "I'm the father of that baby!" His laugh was the voice of crows.

"You are not the father!" Rosetti said. He held the pitchfork with both hands, leveled at Flannery's chest. "You are from Hell—and to there you will return!"

With a powerful thrust, Nicholas Rosetti drove the pitchfork into the priest's chest. The man, still laughing, fell over backward and lay in the dirt of the front yard, silenced.

His blank eyes stared up at the heavens.

"Go straight to Hell!" Rosetti said.

91

With great effort, Nicholas Rosetti carried the girl out of the barn. Colleen tucked her face under his chin, turning herself completely over to his protection. She was so young, and so very close to giving birth.

"He was lying," said Colleen. "He's not the father of this child. I swear it. You have to believe me."

"I know that, Colleen. Don't trouble yourself. You must be strong for the baby's sake."

Rosetti directed his next comments to Justin, who was following close behind him. "Sister Katherine wasn't strong enough," he said as they crossed the barnyard. "We have to be strong, Justin. Yesterday I told you I trusted you. I do trust you. I trust no one but you and myself. Watch the body of Father Flannery. If it's necessary, *kill Father Flannery again!*"

Entering the cottage, Justin had a feeling of vertigo. The living room looked different. A big mahogany grandfather clock that reached to the beams was ticking somberly. It hadn't been there before.

My God, he had just watched the murder of a priest. He'd done nothing to stop it. Why?

Because he believed in evil? Because he was surrounded by it? Because Hell was right here on earth?

"The Beavier child should be born quietly, too. Out of the public eye, just like this one," Rosetti muttered. "The crowds in Rome—a terrible mistake."

"Why are we here?" Justin asked. "Why Colleen?"

"I have the same question, Father. We'll see very soon."

Bending low to avoid the heavy ceiling beams, Rosetti and Justin entered a small room off the kitchen. Justin turned back the threadbare bed coverings. He helped ease the pregnant girl onto the bed.

"*Oooh,* it's terrible," Colleen cried. She clutched at the crucifix that hung from a chain around her neck.

Rosetti motioned to Justin. "Will you get me my stole? Also the manual."

Colleen was having intense contractions. Her face looked almost anemic, and her body was covered in sweat. Justin could see movement in the swell of her belly beneath the blankets.

"Where is the doctor?" he asked suddenly. "Why isn't the doctor here yet?"

Rosetti's eyes narrowed. "*We* are going to deliver the child," he whispered. "No one else will know it has been born."

92

The skies over Rome had never been so dark and foreboding. Streaks of lightning stabbed the city. Rain fell in torrents.

The delivery room inside Salvator Mundi Hospital was calm and vast and sparklingly clean. It must have seemed as scary as a morgue to Kathleen, though. It certainly did to me.

But Kathleen seemed all right now. She had screamed and lost control when the pope had entered her room, but now she was herself again. She had no memory of his visit or her terrified, violent reaction to him.

A nervous group of Salvatorian Sisters in immaculate white uniforms and starched, veil-like headdresses were assisting the special team of doctors. Kathleen's mother and father visited, but neither seemed comfortable in the birthing room. Nor did Kathleen want them there.

"You're staying, Anne?" she asked me as soon as they left.

"Of course. As long as you want me here."

As two of the nuns transferred her from the bed to the sterile white delivery table, Kathleen closed her eyes. The nurses gently placed her feet in cold metal obstetric stirrups. This was it.

They swiveled down a mirror so that she could watch herself. She looked into her own eyes, and I wondered what she saw there.

"No! Please!" Kathleen suddenly shouted.

"It's all right, Kathleen. Everything is fine so far," she heard a calming male voice tell her.

We both turned to where the voice had come from.

A good-looking man in loose-fitting white scrubs stood there, his dark brown eyes sparkling with amusement. A harsh light was glinting behind him. It almost seemed to be winking out of the doctor's right eye.

"I am Dr. Annunziata. You remember me? We met last night in your room. I would like to give you something to help with the delivery, Kathleen. What we call an epidural. Okay?"

Kathleen answered with a gut-wrenching moan. "I don't feel well. I think something's wrong. It feels bad in my stomach. Really bad. Like there are more babies than one."

Dr. Annunziata nodded sympathetically. "Just one baby, I promise. Believe it or not, everything is absolutely perfect so far. You are in glowing health, a wonderful condition to have a beautiful baby."

"I hope so," Kathleen whispered.

A second doctor pierced a long sharp needle into her back. It hurt me just to watch the needle go into Kathleen.

Then Kathleen saw that I was looking on from behind a white gauze mask. "You won't leave? No matter what?" she asked.

"No matter what," I promised and gently patted her. I couldn't leave if I wanted to. I had a job to do here.

Maybe an unspeakable one.

"You're going to have a beautiful baby, Kathleen," Dr. Annunziata said. "This is my four thousand three hundred sixty-fourth baby. Did you know that? Absolutely true.

"Nothing to it," the doctor whispered beguilingly to Kathleen. "Nothing can possibly go wrong."

93

No one could possibly understand how she felt. Kathleen still couldn't believe any of this was happening to her. In that way, nothing had changed since the abortion clinic in Boston. She squeezed her eyes shut hard.

It was brighter and more vivid behind her eyelids than in the hospital delivery room. She felt as if she were being lifted, then carried far away from Salvator Mundi. Her baby was insignificant in the sweep of the universe and infinite time.

I am in so far over my head. This is so horrible. It must be a nightmare.

What is happening? Oh, my God, am I dying? she thought. *Please, let me wake up from this.*

"It's time to push," Anne said, and that brought Kathleen back to the present for an instant. Father Rosetti had told her to trust Anne, no matter what happened. She did. Anne was the only one she trusted. Anne was the best person here, the most solid, the most kind. There was almost something motherly about her, even though she was just a few years older than Kathleen.

Through eyes opened only a slit, a scene came to Kathleen in a rush. *It was nine months ago. It was the night of the dance, February 23.*

She remembered everything as if it were happening all over again.

Her dress, the pale green satin Monique Lhuillier that she had begged her mother to buy for her in Boston, was crumpled up underneath her breasts. There was a terrible weight on her chest. She could hardly breathe.

She saw herself in the speedy yellow Mercedes. Yes, she remembered that. Jamie was driving, and he looked Hollywood gorgeous. She could see every detail of his face and hair, and the way he looked at her. His good looks scared her, but they thrilled her, too.

The car had a leather interior and a gleaming instrument panel. The radio was blaring Kanye, then Drake.

And then everything had changed—just like that.

They stopped to park, and he wanted more than she was ready to give. He *expected* it. Like she *owed* him. But she didn't, and now she didn't even want him to touch her. Jamie started yelling at her over the pounding bass. He was saying things she couldn't bear—she was a dick tease, a frigid bitch—and so she held her hands over her ears.

They were at pitch-black Sachuest Point and it was late at night. No one was around but the two of them.

"I told you *no!*" she finally yelled back at him. "No means *no.* Please, Jamie. Listen to what I'm saying. Don't you dare touch me! Take me home. Now!"

Then Jamie went insane. Kathleen felt a rough hand mauling her chest, another grabbing at her between her legs. Jamie's voice was suddenly much deeper, scarier. He outweighed her by a hundred pounds and he was nothing but muscle.

She was terrified now. So helpless in the dark, deserted park.

She didn't know what to do or how to stop him. She bit down hard into the back of his outstretched hand, and Jamie screamed in pain.

He threw the door open on her side and pushed at her roughly. He was yelling obscenities at her, his face beet-red.

"Walk home, Ice Queen! Walk, you cunt!"

Suddenly, another car pulled up in the lovers' lane. Two boys got out, staggering a little. They were drunk or stoned or both. She knew them. It was Peter Thompson and Chris Raleigh. Had they been following behind the Mercedes?

Were they here to help her? Or hurt her?

Kathleen stumbled onto the crunching, frozen roadside. The raw smell of ocean filled her nose. Her body tingled from the biting cold.

Jamie and the two other boys came up from behind. Jamie lunged at her. She'd never seen anyone so angry in her life. The other two boys were almost as bad.

She didn't want to remember any more of this.

She didn't want to remember Jamie Jordan and what had really happened at Sachuest Point.

"Push, Kathleen," she heard.

94

Sweat ran off Justin's forehead in rivulets. It was hot and dank and close in the small bedroom. It was also the most intimate experience Justin had ever had—to be present at a human birth, to watch this young girl deliver her baby.

He kept hearing the words over and over in his mind: *If you can't believe there can be a miracle now, a divine birth, how can you say that you ever believed?*

Colleen Galaher's contractions were coming every few seconds. She was working hard to deliver the child. He was right there with her.

Justin wondered if the sixteen-year-old girl had been in any way prepared for the pain. He certainly hadn't been, and it wasn't even his to feel. She cried out and clutched the sheets, her face an expression of agony—and then, in the moment she wasn't contracting, she became almost peaceful again.

He was humbled and awed by the experience. He felt tender

and loving toward the patiently suffering girl. But most of all, he felt blessed.

"Push," he heard Father Rosetti urge.

If you can't believe there can be a miracle now...

But he could, by God, he did believe!

He wondered what was happening in Rome. He was terribly afraid for Kathleen and Anne. If anything happened to them, he could never forgive himself.

In the last few minutes, a profound change had come over him. He was starting to believe that Colleen was the true virgin, that hers was the true holy child. If that was so, what would happen in Rome? What *was* happening? Had Anne been put in danger by Father Rosetti?

In the small bed with the tattered blankets, the Irish girl cried softly and tried to be brave. The birth of her child was difficult, but it was also the most beautiful thing Justin had ever witnessed in his life.

"Be prepared for anything," he heard Rosetti warn from the other side of the bed. "You're drifting. Stay with us, Justin."

"I'm right here, Father. I'm ready."

"Are you ready for *this?*" Rosetti asked.

As he looked on, a tiny head began to slide from between Colleen's legs. Suddenly, Justin was seeing life in a way he never had before. He understood something fundamental about marriage and love and sex that he'd never comprehended until now.

Justin reached out and gently placed his hand under the child's tiny skull. It had thick dark hair like Jesus's as a man. He was rapt with awe.

"He's here!" Colleen announced in a soft, reverent voice. "He has come."

95

P ush," Kathleen heard.

She *pushed*. God, how she *pushed*. She *pushed* Jamie Jordan away and tried to run as fast as she could for the road out of Sachuest Point.

The long column skirt of her satin dress was slim and restricting. She pulled it up around her waist and ran. Jamie was insane about not getting what he wanted. What was he thinking? What was he doing? What about the other two? Why were they here?

Behind her, both cars accelerated, shooting up sprays of gravel. Were Jamie and his friends heading back to Newport without her?

Oh, my God, it's freezing, Kathleen realized, and she began to panic. *He can't just leave me out here. How can he be so mad? I don't belong to him. He has no right.*

Tears blinded Kathleen. The strong winter wind coming off the ocean blew right through her clothing, blew her beautiful silver headband off her head. Dervishes of powdery snow swirled around her thin-soled shoes.

He has to come back for me. I'll freeze out here. I could die. I will die!

Kathleen slowed to a walk on the crusty dirt road. She had no other choice. This was the only way back to town, and it was miles.

She pointed herself toward the distant pocket of lights that was the city of Newport. Everywhere she looked there was a faint, eerie glow. All around her, the ocean roared like a squadron of low-flying airplanes. No one would hear her screams for help.

One of her feet landed on a sharp rock and she fell, striking the ground hard. She cried out in pain. She had twisted her ankle. Then Kathleen curled herself into a small, safe ball on the ground. That felt better—better than facing the bitter cold.

She wondered if she could sleep right here. Maybe she'd be all right in the morning, if she could just sleep.

No, she would be dead. She'd freeze to death.

How could Jamie and the others leave her out here?

Then Kathleen heard something she dreaded even more than the killing cold.

They were coming back.

Cars sped back down the long stretch of park road. The bright lights flashed through the bare-limbed trees and up the deserted, pitch-black road. Afterimages danced before Kathleen's eyes, looping red and violet rings, waving streaks of silver, like in a dreamy dance hall.

She pushed herself up to a kneeling position. Stones ground into her palms. She brushed off her ripped, stained gown, once so beautiful.

Then a terrible blow from behind came crashing down on her skull.

She was falling, falling, falling into darkness. Where was she?

"She's coming to," she heard. It was Chris Raleigh. He was crouched over her. They all were.

Peter Thompson was running his hands roughly over her chest. Then he slid both breasts out of her dress. His hands were freezing cold.

"No, please," she whispered. "Don't touch me. Please."

Through haze and fog Kathleen saw Jamie's face looming above her. He was holding something in his hand while he moved it back and forth. His face was red; he was blowing with exertion.

Something white spurted from his hand.

Kathleen knew what it was. She saw his swollen penis. Jamie Jordan was coming all over her dress, her skin, her underpants.

"Push," she heard. *"You have to push, Kathleen!"*

Kathleen screamed. She wasn't in Newport! She was in the delivery room in Rome. White masks leaned in closer. Doctors and nurses. Hovering over her.

"It's all right, Kathleen. Just push again. Push."

What was happening? She was going back and forth between two realities—the hospital in Rome and the beach outside Newport. She had no control over the sequence of the scenes.

"Get off me! Get off me! Get away with that thing!" she screamed.

Her underpants were pulled down around her knees. Jamie was rubbing his cum between her legs. She was sticky and wet down there.

Jamie! Jamie had done it.

She finally remembered! She remembered everything as if it had just happened. Jamie had gotten her pregnant at the beach that night.

She *was* a virgin, but the birth of her child couldn't be divine. Could it? Jamie Jordan had gotten her pregnant. She was absolutely sure of it.

There was a cry then.

Whose cry was it? Hers?

Where was she?

Kathleen's eyes suddenly opened wide. Of course—she was here, with her feet in stirrups. She gasped and arched. Her body felt like it was being pulled apart, but there wasn't any pain anymore, just terrible, numbing exhaustion.

She saw blazing kettledrum lights whirling over her head. Then the swarming doctors and nurses, and Anne standing right beside the delivery table.

In the mirror she saw the baby's head emerging. She saw a face, and Kathleen Beavier fainted.

96

Colleen Galaher sobbed softly as she watched sharp sewing scissors floating over her quivering stomach.

What were the two priests doing to her now? She watched as the umbilical cord was carefully tied by Father O'Carroll. Then the exhausted, sweating priest cut the cord. Father Rosetti held her baby.

The girl felt vindicated. She was a true virgin, and here was the child. Now what would happen to them?

The infant was being held up high like a beautiful little lamb, like a chalice at the celebration of the Holy Eucharist, in the priest's strong hands.

She wanted to see his face. She smiled at the thought of it.

She reached out her arms and saw that they were shaking badly. She was incredibly weak; she'd never felt like this before. Of course not; she'd never been a *mother* before.

"Please, Father, let me see?"

Colleen thought that the light slanting in the bedroom window was making a golden robe around the child's shoulders.

Tears were in her eyes. *I am a mother.*

"I want to see. My baby? May I?"

"In a minute, Colleen."

Father Rosetti began to rub the baby's throat in an upward motion with his thumb. He then wiped away mucus with a swab of disinfected linen. He gently flicked the sole of the baby's foot, and it let out a tiny squawk.

"He's alive, healthy," he said softly to the young girl. "He's just fine."

"Let me see him," she pleaded again. "I want to hold my baby."

But Father Rosetti carried the child out of the bedroom. He didn't let the mother touch the infant. He never allowed Colleen Galaher to see her little son's face.

He left Colleen crying.

"Please, my baby. Why won't you let me see my baby?"

97

The two priests hurried from the lonely cottage to their car. *We must look like kidnappers,* Justin thought. And maybe they were.

"Father, wait," he called ahead to Rosetti. "What about the girl? Poor Colleen?"

But Rosetti was already running with the child wrapped in his arms. He folded himself into the backseat of the car.

"You drive, Father. Woodbine Seminary. Just go straight."

"The girl? Colleen?" Justin insisted.

"We'll get help for her at Woodbine. *Drive!* Do as I tell you."

Hands shaking, Justin obeyed.

The car accelerated down the rocky dirt road twisting away from the forlorn cottage. It carried Father Justin O'Carroll; it carried the chief investigator for the Congregation of Sacred Rites, who was gently cradling the infant.

Justin's mind burned with questions. What were they to do with the child? What plan did Father Rosetti have?

What was the truth about Colleen Galaher's baby? And Kathleen's in Rome? He had a bad feeling about this—a terrible feeling.

Justin felt like he was living a nightmare that wouldn't end. Why was he here in this car? He was kidnapping a young girl's baby. He had left the poor girl alone moments after she gave birth.

"*Father Rosetti!* I can't do this."

"Drive, damn you! You are under orders from the Holy Father in Rome. Obey them. *Drive!*"

They rode past rundown farms on the road toward the seminary in Costelloe. Past vast stubbled fields of barley and potatoes. Past a clique of frowning men standing around a crippled donkey cart and a young woman in a mackintosh and plastic bonnet—a girl who reminded Justin of Colleen.

He turned toward the backseat. "Father?" he asked again. "What about the poor girl?"

Rosetti refused to answer. He was off in his own world, and he wouldn't take his eyes off the face of the baby.

They rose up a curving road onto a wild moor. Smoking fog began to curl from the ground, shredding as the speeding car blew through it. The sky was dark and threatening.

Terrible fear began to bloom in Justin's chest. He couldn't catch his breath. He turned, trying to peek inside the blanket at the same time. He saw nothing except the baby's dark curls.

"Where exactly is this Woodbine Seminary that we're headed to?" Justin asked.

"Straight ahead. Close. I told you. Drive."

Just then the road turned toward the Atlantic Ocean and past a small wooden sign: WOODBINE 7 KM.

"Woodbine," he said, relieved that there was such a place.

As Justin nervously steered the sedan along limestone cliffs over the ocean, he heard Rosetti praying in Latin. *"Requiem aeternam dona eis."*

Justin's hands locked tightly on the steering wheel.

He froze. The hairs on his neck stood.

He recognized the holy prayers of the Anointing of the Sick.

The Roman Catholic prayers for the seriously ill or just deceased.

Prayers for those in danger of death.

Justin stepped down hard on the brakes.

The car fishtailed to the left. The front grille effortlessly sheared away a row of baby scrub pines. The tires screamed.

The car continued its full 360-degree turn, rolling over gnarled bushes and rocks, finally smacking hard into a full-grown fir tree.

Justin's forehead smashed against the windshield. His head rolled to one side and then slumped down onto his chest.

Out of the corner of a bloodied eye, he saw a quick, bounding movement.

Rosetti was plunging out of the car's back door. A small bundle of pink blanket was clutched in one of his arms. The baby was wailing.

Justin had to save it.

98

Justin reeled from the car and stumbled after Rosetti and Colleen Galaher's baby. The cold sea air whipped at his body and his face. The sky was getting darker, and the wind made a shrill, high-pitched wail.

"Father! Father, stop! Where are you going? Father Rosetti!" Justin screamed. "Stop, you son of a bitch. You murderer!"

He ran forward, straining his muscles and clutching his burning chest. Up ahead, the baby began to cry.

The Atlantic Ocean came into view as he made it to the top of a bare promontory, a pointing finger of black rocks and boulders. The height and the sheer drop off the dark cliff took Justin's breath away.

It was three hundred feet straight down to where great rollers thundered over rocks as sharp as teeth.

There were birds all over the ocean, thousands of birds screeching louder than he'd ever heard.

"Dear God!" he shouted. "What is happening here?"

He tottered across a foot-wide ledge to the next plateau of rock. The harsh wind sliced right through his clothes. He painfully hoisted himself over a loose molar of shale slanting into the cliffs at a sixty-degree angle.

A sheen of cold sweat coated his forehead. He felt as if his lungs were going to burst. *God, make me strong.*

Thirty feet above him, the black-clad figure of Rosetti stood perched on another weathered rock face. High over his head the sky was filled with birds. Everything was becoming dark beneath them. Night in the middle of the day.

Justin saw a flash of the pink blanket. The child. The poor baby continued to cry.

"Father, stop—please. You can't be sure. Are you sure?"

"You don't *believe* anymore." Rosetti's powerful voice echoed down the steep cliffside. "None of you believe! Not in Our Lord! Not in Satan! Not in anything that matters!"

Rosetti was holding the child loosely in one powerful arm. They were both leaning out over the edge of the rocks.

Justin had a blinding thought. It made him ill. *Rosetti could be Satan himself. How do I know otherwise? Satan could right now be holding the Savior of mankind.*

He had to see the child's face. That was his mission. It was why he was here, wasn't it?

He saw Rosetti lift the infant high in the air with both huge hands. The priest's eyes were like empty black holes as he stared down on Justin.

Above the cliff, the birds were swooping in. Thousands of birds careened wildly in every direction. The noise of their screeches and calls was deafening.

Justin was so afraid he could scarcely breathe. Something unearthly was happening. His ears were ringing and starting to ache.

Nicholas Rosetti's voice was harsh and barely recognizable.

"This is the Beast! Have no doubt of it, Justin. All the signs in the prediction of Fátima have been met. The Virgin has guided me to this very spot, with this child. This is the Beast! Satan is so wise, so clever, the girl herself never knew. Do you find that so difficult to believe? Is it not possible for you to believe anything on faith? Do you believe in your God, Father? Only your faith will save you now, for you are in grave danger. All of these foul black birds—they are devils. Fallen angels. The *child* commands them. The *child* has called them here."

Justin couldn't take his eyes away from the helpless infant. He couldn't just believe. He had to *see*.

"Who are you?" he shouted at Rosetti, straining to be heard over the pounding waves and screaming birds.

"Suppose I told you I was Michael the Archangel? Would that satisfy you? Fine, then, I'm *Michael!* I am Michael. Believe it if you must."

"Let me see the child. You said you trusted me. Let me see, Father."

Above them, the mountainside rose another two hundred feet. The uppermost rocks seemed to pierce the clouds. More black birds circled, screeching angrily. Screaming down at Rosetti. Were they the legions? Was Rosetti telling the truth about the devils? And the child who commanded them?

Justin shielded his eyes and called up to Rosetti again. "How can you be sure? How do you know that you aren't holding an innocent baby? Father? I see no sign."

"Must you always *see* to believe? How can you be sure that Jesus Christ became man?" Rosetti's voice rang out angrily. "How can you be sure that Jesus has redeemed our souls from the eternal fires of Hell?"

"Has he?" Justin called back. "Has he redeemed us from Hell? It seems that the gates of Hell are wide open right now."

"It's their time, their turn. Unless we stop them. They don't have power on Earth yet. They can act only through humans. This child is human."

The idea was monstrous—but it was consistent with everything Justin had ever read about the fallen angels.

Great waves of nausea washed over him. Was he engaged in a dialogue with the Devil? Was he siding with Satan against everything good and holy in the world? What did Father Rosetti know? What was he holding in his arms?

He knew he couldn't look down at the spinning vortex tempting him, trying to pull him off the cliffs.

Once again he hollered above the crashing sea, above the piercing cries of gulls and crows and gannets clouding over the cliffside. He screamed above the cries of the devils, "We can go to the Woodbine Seminary! We can perform an exorcism. Father! We can talk. You know what I'm saying is best!"

As Justin gazed skyward, he saw Rosetti's broad shoulders sag forward. The priest moved a step back, away from the edge of the rocks. Dark yellow bile began dripping from the corners of his mouth. Blood ran from his nose. Was he dying?

"Come up here, Father," the Vatican priest said in an oddly quiet voice. "If you must, come to me. Come see the child for yourself."

Justin took a single step forward on the loose, shifting rocks. The sea winds flogged his face. Something warned him not to go any higher. *No closer to Rosetti and the child. No higher on the dark, slippery rocks.*

But he took step after step on the steep stones. His arms felt like blocks of lead. He was afraid he wouldn't be able to hold the baby if he reached Rosetti. He was afraid that he was about to die, not ever knowing the truth of the virgin births.

Justin's leaden feet moved upward, as if against his will.

When he finally looked up again, he was staring into the burning eyes of Nicholas Rosetti.

"You want to see? Then look, Justin O'Carroll. Feast your eyes. Look at the child! *Look!*"

99

Kathleen uttered the words in a soft, barely audible whisper. "My baby's all right? Is my baby all right? Doctor?"

It was the voice of a frightened seventeen-year-old girl. The voice of a new mother.

Kathleen tried to get a better look at the dark, slick child, its limbs still curled tight. The doctor was holding the baby at the far end of the birthing table. She strained to see its face.

"Is anything the matter?" I asked Dr. Annunziata in a low whisper.

"No, no. Of course not," he muttered, but I wasn't sure whether to believe him. He was acting very strange.

Meanwhile, the other doctors and nurses from Salvator Mundi were watching the mother and child in awed, almost reverent silence. The Swiss Guards stood at the ready, waiting for a sign. They still seemed tense. What had they been expecting? What were their orders? They were *armed*. Were they present to protect Kathleen and the child? Or was there another reason?

The chief obstetrician lightly rubbed the baby with a towel to help clear the airway. The tiny infant obligingly began to scream, an unmistakable, anguished, and *human* sound.

Dr. Annunziata finally smiled. The roomful of medical and Church people smiled at the naturalness of the child's response. Even some of the Swiss Guards loosened up and grinned.

I tried to think positively as well. The baby was like us. The baby was human. The baby was beautiful and good. A new life had come into the world, and that was always a miracle.

But was this birth a *sign* as well? Had it been promised a hundred years before at Fátima?

I moved closer to Dr. Annunziata. "*Is* there a problem, Doctor?"

He looked at me. "No, not really a problem. But there is a... a situation."

100

Nicholas Rosetti felt a sudden calm, and he wondered if it was another trick being played on him. Soon he would be relieved of his great burden for the first time since his meeting with Pope Pius. He had done his job, his investigation. He believed he had found out the truth.

"I need to know." Justin O'Carroll was calling above the howling winds and the cries of the seabirds.

Only love and pity made Rosetti address the young priest. "If you have no faith, then believe this," he said. "Believe *medicine*. Believe *science*. Listen to me. Colleen Galaher was christened *Colin Galaher*. Born with two sets of sexual organs. Her doctor in town did what he could."

"I don't understand," Justin said, waving his hand toward the child. "What are you saying?"

"Colleen Galaher has *no ovaries*," Rosetti said hoarsely. "They were removed."

Rosetti held the baby aloft. He spoke in an agonized voice, nearly incomprehensible. "This baby is the Devil's own. This baby will change the world."

A muffled cry rose out of the pink blanket. A *baby's* cry.

Doubt flooded Justin's mind. Who could he believe now? The Devil was clever, and he was everywhere.

The wind quickly swallowed the baby's howl as the birds hovered everywhere around Father Rosetti. They looked as if they wanted to swoop down and carry away the infant.

Justin heard a tortured cry from above. "Pray for me, Father O'Carroll."

With trembling hands, the Vatican priest slowly opened the woolen blanket. His lips moved in prayer as he crossed the baby's forehead with the side of his thumb. The infant screamed in pain and struggled fiercely.

Then Father Rosetti opened the blanket and showed the baby to Justin.

Justin stared into the child's eyes—and thousands of eyes stared back. He could clearly see countless eyes inside those of the child's.

The legions were right there.

Justin stumbled backward, almost losing his footing on the rock. His heart thundered. At first he had seen a child's face, but then it changed before his eyes. It became the face of the fiercest animal, then several animals in one, and it roared at him. It tried to scare him away, and it nearly succeeded.

The sound was hideous, unearthly. The *thing* shook furiously, with great strength, and then bit into Rosetti's cheek with long, sharp teeth when the priest wouldn't release his grip. The animal— the Beast—screamed and raged. All of the devils inside the infant seemed to cry out at once.

The priest didn't pull away. Nicholas Rosetti held the Beast right up to his face.

"You saw it, Justin. The eyes, the legions. You know. Now go back to Rome. The true virgin is there. Please pray for me."

And then Rosetti stepped right off the high cliff. The priest and infant fell together. They seemed suspended by an invisible cord for a moment. The infant continued to struggle, to cling with its teeth to Rosetti's cheek.

The birds flew all around the falling priest. Their wings whirred like thousands of rotor blades. Shrieking, they seemed to be trying to catch Father Rosetti, to break his fall.

But they couldn't.

Rosetti and the child clapped the cold, choppy water and disappeared beneath the dark and turbulent waves. A thick column of smoke rose from the sea. The water hissed and churned.

The birds all over the mountain shrieked louder than ever as they swooped in a great black cloud to the sea below. They changed shapes—became flying wolves. They dove into the waves.

They did not resurface.

Justin finally dropped to the rocks of the high cliffside, where he sobbed uncontrollably. *"Requiem aeternam dona eis."* He prayed for the eternal soul of Nicholas Rosetti and for his own soul as well.

He had seen the face of Satan.

101

I was keenly aware of the strange, sudden quiet that had fallen over the hospital room. First the silence, then the laughter, and then...silence again.

The doctors, the Salvator Mundi nurses, and the technicians stood still, gazing with awed eyes as they watched the infant's first awkward moves—as if they were experiencing the most important and beautiful moment of their lives.

I trembled. Felt my heart knocking in my chest like a fist.

You are the strongest of all of us. Over and over, I heard the words of Father Rosetti the last time we'd spoken.

Anne, the Beast must be killed.

I was on the verge of panic when I heard my name spoken. The voice was deep and resonant.

I looked up at the doctor who stood nearest to me. *He hadn't said a word.*

I turned toward a dark-haired technician monitoring the EKG machine. *The voice wasn't his, either.*

The voice came again. Louder. Surer. Nearer.

Anne, it called to me. *It must die—or we will. An eternity of suffering for mankind. Kill the Beast, Anne! Kill the child now!*

I moved closer to the doctor. Closer to the child. My body quivered and shook.

In the name of the Father, kill the child of evil!

We were promised a clear sign at the moment of the divine birth—that's what Father Rosetti had said. It was a matter of faith.

But did I have faith? And why me? Why had I been chosen to be in Rome?

I recited simple prayers from my childhood. *Hail Mary. Glory be to the Father.*

I heard the deep voice again.

In the name of the Father, and of the Son, and of the Holy Spirit—KILL THE CHILD!

My hands were trembling and my legs felt so weak I could barely stand. Still, I took another step closer to the infant.

I saw a table of sharp metal instruments gleaming by the bed. There was a scalpel I could use.

I nearly fainted at the thought.

You must, Anne. That's why you're here.

"Give him to me." I finally spoke, hearing my own voice as if it were someone else's. "Let me hold the child. Let me give him to Kathleen."

As I reached out my arms, Dr. Annunziata suddenly turned and handed the child over to a nurse.

Something in the doctor's eyes gave me pause. Who was he? Did we have him checked out? I couldn't remember.

He spoke quietly to me, confidentially. I heard the regret in his tone. "This is not a holy child," he said. "But he is still a child of God."

At this, the cajoling voice in my head stopped abruptly.

And I knew, as clear as sunlight, that Annunziata spoke the truth.

This infant wasn't the Savior. But it was an innocent baby.

The nurse holding the baby swaddled it in a clean blanket in a few deft movements. Then she presented the baby to Kathleen.

Kathleen took the child into her arms as she wept with happiness and relief. I saw that the baby had the same blue eyes as Kathleen.

She looked into the baby's sweet face, and I could see a mother's love wash over her. "My son," she said. "My baby boy."

Yes, I believed that. I believed in the mother and her child. And I believed that my investigation was finished.

102

It was finally over for me. And the suffering was apparently over for countless others.

That night, rain fell in drought-stricken India; sick children stopped streaming into hospitals in Boston, Los Angeles, and elsewhere; and the plagues that had ravaged China and Africa suddenly, miraculously ended.

It would be someone else's job to decode and demystify everything that had happened.

Not mine.

What I wanted to know was what had happened in Ireland. But I couldn't reach Justin. And there was no word from Rome.

A room had been reserved for me at a nearby hotel, and I decided to walk there from the hospital. I was bone-tired, but I didn't think I could sleep.

I tried to stay off the main streets for fear I might be recognized. I didn't even know the name of the narrow cobblestone alley where

I was walking, but it didn't really matter. I wanted to be alone, and I was.

Suddenly, I was driven to my knees by a hard blow to the center of my back. The pain was terrible. I looked around but saw no one.

My body began to shake, and the shaking wouldn't stop.

A deep voice spoke to me and I could smell its hot, stinking breath.

You failed your Church, Anne. You failed again.

"I did what was right," I protested. "I didn't fail!"

I was struck again, even harder than the first time. Then I was pressed facedown into the dusky cobblestones of the street. I tasted dirt and then my own blood. I was petrified.

You're worthless. And now it's your turn to die. You can join Father Rosetti and Father O'Carroll in Hell.

"No!" I yelled as loudly as I could with my nose and mouth jammed into stone. "They're not dead. I would know it if Justin was gone!"

I took another incredible blow; it was as if a bat had struck my head and neck.

I touched the place where I'd been struck. *No blood!*

"You can't hurt me!" I yelled, even louder this time.

Suddenly, I wasn't afraid. I picked myself up and I stared defiantly at where the Voice seemed to emanate.

"Where are you? Why don't you show yourself? *Coward!*" I yelled.

There was a flash of light. Nicholas Rosetti stood before me where no one had been a moment before.

He was on his feet, but I could tell that he was dead. His skin was waxy and pale and blue in places. His eyes showed no movement. But the Voice came from his mouth, like a cheap ventriloquist's trick.

Rosetti is dead. Now do you believe?

I looked at poor Father Rosetti in sorrow and shock, and then Justin was standing where the priest had been. Justin looked more flushed than Rosetti. Was he alive?

Do you believe I can't hurt you, Anne? the Voice crooned. *Haven't I already?*

"Yes, yes. In the name of GOD, I do believe that," I yelled. "You can't!"

I walked toward Justin and tears were streaming from my eyes. I kept going, and when I got to him I slowly reached out my hand.

Justin was gone before I could touch him.

"You have no power over me!" I screamed. The street was deserted. "Be gone! You can't hurt me. Go! Damn you, go!"

I stood my ground. I *was* strong. Father Rosetti was right about that.

And then I swooned. I dropped to the street like a sack of wet sand. But it was more than a faint. It was a powerful loss of consciousness, like nothing I had ever experienced.

It was like I was dying.

103

My eyes opened.

I felt a stirring inside my body. It was painful, like a cramp, but then it vanished, and I felt the deepest calm. I knew that a miracle had happened.

It had happened to me.

And I finally understood why I had been called into all this, why I was here.

I was a virgin, and I was pregnant.

104

The following morning, I awoke to a ringing cell phone.

It was Justin.

My heart started to pound. "Oh, Just—" I began.

"I'm here," he interrupted. "Can I come up?"

Tears filled my eyes. He was alive and he was in Rome. Worry left me in such a rush that my body shook. "Yes. Come now," I said.

I hurried and splashed water on my face and ran a brush through my hair. My stomach felt funny, but I needed no new sign that I was pregnant. I was certain of it now. The night before I'd taken a home pregnancy test. It was positive.

When he knocked, I threw open the door, even though I was still wearing my ratty old nightgown. I almost fell into his arms.

And that's when I really let myself go. The tears that hadn't fallen before came in a salty rush. We hugged, and then he kissed me. If there had been even the smallest doubt in my mind that I loved him, it was gone.

I pulled away so I could see him better. I almost couldn't believe that I'd gone twenty-three years without feeling what I did now. It was such a long time not to experience love. There had to be a reason, and now I thought I knew what it was.

"More than anything," Justin whispered, "I missed you. I was so afraid I would never see you again. I dreaded that more than dying in Ireland."

"I'm so glad you're back," I said.

"Me too."

"Kathleen's child isn't the Savior, Justin. Kathleen isn't the virgin mother."

"I know," he said. "Father Rosetti told me what he knew during our last few hours together. He's dead. He died horribly, and so did Colleen's child."

"What?" I gasped.

He shook his head. "The child was the Beast."

There was a time in my life that I wouldn't have been able to comprehend a sentence like that. But now I knew what he meant, and I knew it was true.

Abruptly I told Justin about my pregnancy. I held my breath as I waited to see what his reaction would be. As much as we'd gone through together, it was so much more to ask of him.

My whole future—with or without him—was riding on what he would say next.

Justin stared at me in shock...and joy. "Rosetti said that the true virgin was here in Rome. He meant *you*, Anne. He said that the message of Fátima was that there would be more than one virgin mother, and that one woman would bear the Savior, one would bear the Beast."

"Colleen?" I asked, stunned. "She isn't dead? She's all right?"

"I brought Colleen to Woodbine Seminary. She's being cared

for there. I saw Satan, Anne. The eyes of the legions of fallen angels were in the eyes of Colleen's child. Thousands of eyes, and all of them filled with hatred and evil. Like nothing I've ever seen or imagined."

"Hold me," I whispered, and Justin did.

"I love you so much, Anne." He told me what I already felt so strongly.

"I love you, too, Justin. But what do we do about it?"

He knelt before me and softly bowed his head. "I love you with my heart and soul. I know that I'll love you for eternity. I have to leave the priesthood. Then, will you please marry me?" he asked.

I knelt and faced Justin. I wanted to be as close to him as I possibly could be. I needed to stare directly into his beautiful eyes.

"Yes," I said. "Yes, yes, and *yes*."

105

Nine months later. Brigham and Women's Hospital, Boston, Massachusetts.

Who can tell about the ways of God? Who can truly understand? I certainly can't.

The tiniest, most precious baby lay in my arms. The child was only moments old, eyes open and staring directly into mine, holding my gaze. Not a thousand eyes, just two beautiful blue ones. It was a perfect child, but I didn't need the doctors to tell me that.

I knew. I just knew.

Dr. Maria Ruocco leaned in close to me. She was a lovely woman, but not commissioned by the Church to be here. Gently, she brushed the hair away from my face. I saw something in her expression. This doctor, who had confidently delivered thousands of children, was confused.

She furrowed her brow, then spoke. "Anne," she said, with hushed reverence. "You were still *intact*."

"I know," I said.

The baby whimpered, cried, nuzzled into my chest. I let down the front of my gown and gave the infant my breast. I thanked God. I didn't completely understand, but I knew this was good. This was right. It was nine months since I had suddenly and mysteriously received the incredible gift. I had conceived without having sex. And now I held a healthy baby in my arms.

Justin stood close to me, his scrub mask hanging around his neck, his handsome face beaming. His eyes were filled with love for me and love for the child. He had proved himself in a thousand ways while I was pregnant. I loved him even more now than I had that day in Rome.

And he believed—we both believed in this miracle before our eyes.

I didn't know what would happen after I left the hospital room, what the child's life would be like, or mine either. But I knew happiness on this day. I never wanted it to end.

I stared down at this child—this holy child—this baby girl, Noelle.

The Savior of us all was a girl.

EPILOGUE
NOELLE, NOELLE

106

Noelle was eighteen years old when she witnessed the car accident on Vandemeer Avenue. She was living with her brothers and sisters and her mother and father, the O'Carroll clan, in a small town in Maine.

She ran to the crash without thinking. She was studying to become a doctor because she wanted to do as much good as she could. She'd learned that from her parents: They taught at the University of Maine, but they also operated a halfway house for homeless kids. They'd always been loving, caring parents, and they were beloved by the whole town.

Noelle had never seen anything as horrible as the crash at the usually quiet Vandemeer Avenue intersection—not in her whole life.

The yellow Volvo station wagon had struck a chestnut tree. The unyielding tree had split open the vehicle, passing through the engine block, through the front and back seats.

The driver and his young wife died instantly. Three small children in the back also appeared to be dead.

It was so needless, so tragic.

A fourth child, an adorable little girl in footie pajamas, had been thrown free of the car. She was lying, badly injured, on someone's lawn.

The girl, crying softly, was being attended to by men and women from the neighborhood who had rushed to the accident scene.

Noelle could stand the carnage no longer. It made her so angry that these people had died. She turned away from the unbearable sadness, from the earsplitting wails of approaching police cars and ambulances.

Her head ached. She couldn't bear it. She had to do something to help the family.

She knelt down on the edge of the road, across the street from the smoldering wreck. She bowed her head and prayed with all her heart. *Make the family whole again,* she thought.

She didn't know if she could do it. But she *saw* them alive and well in her mind.

She looked up at the girl on the lawn—and nothing had happened.

Let this family live. They deserve a second chance. Let them have it, she prayed. *Come back to life. Come to life, little children. Come back to life, mother and father.*

And then, a moment later, she heard cries coming from near the car.

"They're alive. All of them. They're alive!"

She let out the breath she'd been holding. She'd brought the family back to life, just as Jesus raised Lazarus out of love and compassion.

It was the first of Noelle's miracles. As she watched the children, the mother and father, her heart leaped with joy and she was filled with a sense of purpose.

She hurried away so as not to be noticed. She had no way of knowing that she was being watched.

The eyes hungrily followed Noelle up the pretty tree-lined street. All the way to her home. They were the fathomless eyes of a boy who'd been washed up cold and hungry on a beach eighteen years before. A boy who'd been thrown into the cold Atlantic Ocean and survived.

There was a faint red mark on the young man's forehead, a cross made with the fingernail of a man of God.

The mark always burned, and it kept his hatred focused.

He'd waited all these years. He had been patient. But now, as he watched Noelle and her family, he meant to take what was rightfully his.

He watched her—with thousands of vengeful, bestial eyes.

FIND OUT HOW
THE CONFESSIONS
BEGAN...

AND WHAT REALLY
HAPPENED TO
MALCOLM AND
MAUD ANGEL.

TURN THE PAGE FOR A PREVIEW.

CONFESSIONS OF A MURDER SUSPECT

JAMES PATTERSON

AND MAXINE PAETRO

1

I have some really bad secrets to share with someone, and it might as well be you—a stranger, a reader of books, but most of all, a person who can't hurt me. So here goes nothing, or maybe everything. I'm not sure if I can even tell the difference anymore.

The night my parents died—after they'd been carried out in slick black body bags through the service elevator—my brother Matthew shouted at the top of his powerful lungs, "My parents were vile, but they didn't deserve to be taken out with the *trash*!"

He was right about the last part—and, as things turned out, the first part as well.

But I'm getting ahead of myself, aren't I? Please forgive me....I do that a lot.

I'd been asleep downstairs, directly under my parents' bedroom, when it happened. So I never heard a thing—no frantic thumping, no terrified shouting, no fracas at all. I woke up to the scream of sirens speeding up Central Park West, maybe one of the most common sounds in New York City.

But that night it was different.

The sirens stopped *right downstairs*. That was what caused me to wake up with a hundred-miles-an-hour heartbeat. Was the building on fire? Did some old neighbor have a stroke?

I threw off my double layer of blankets, went to my window, and looked down to the street, nine dizzying floors below. I saw three police cruisers and what could have been an unmarked police car parked on Seventy-second Street, right at the front gates of our apartment building, the exclusive and infamous Dakota.

A moment later our intercom buzzed, a jarring *blat-blat* that punched right through my flesh and bones.

Why was the doorman paging *us*? This was *crazy*.

My bedroom was the one closest to the front door, so I bolted through the living room, hooked a right at the sharks in the aquarium coffee table, and passed between Robert and his nonstop TV.

When I reached the foyer, I stabbed at the intercom button to stop the irritating blare before it woke up the whole house.

I spoke in a loud whisper to the doorman through the speaker: "Sal? What's happening?"

"Miss Tandy? Two policemen are on the way up to your apartment right now. I couldn't stop them. They got a nine-one-one call. It's an emergency. That's what they said."

"There's been a mistake, Sal. Everyone is asleep here. It's after midnight. How could you let them up?"

Before Sal could answer, the doorbell rang, and then fists pounded the door. A harsh masculine voice called out, "This is the police."

I made sure the chain was in place and then opened the door—but just a crack.

I peered out through the opening and saw two men in the hallway. The older one was as big as a bear but kind of soft-looking and spongy. The younger one was wiry and had a sharp, expressionless face, something like a hatchet blade, or...no, a hatchet blade is exactly right.

The younger one flashed his badge and said, "Sergeant

Capricorn Caputo and Detective Ryan Hayes, NYPD. Please open the door."

Capricorn Caputo? I thought. *Seriously?* "You've got the wrong apartment," I said. "No one here called the police."

"Open the door, miss. And I mean *right now*."

"I'll get my parents," I said through the crack. I had no idea that my parents were dead and that we would be the only serious suspects in a double homicide. I was in my last moment of innocence.

But who am I kidding? No one in the Angel family was ever innocent.

"*Open up,* or my partner will kick down the door!"
Hatchet Face called out.

It is no exaggeration to say that my whole family was
about to get a wake-up call from *hell*. But all I was thinking at that particular moment was that the police could
not kick down the door. This was the *Dakota*. We could
get *evicted* for allowing someone to disturb the peace.

I unlatched the chain and swung the door open. I was
wearing pajamas, of course; chick-yellow ones with dino-
saurs chasing butterflies. Not exactly what I would have
chosen for a meeting with the police.

Detective Hayes, the bearish one, said, "What's your
name?"

5

"Tandy Angel."

"Are you the daughter of Malcolm and Maud Angel?"

"I am. Can you please tell me why you're here?"

"Tandy is your real name?" he said, ignoring my question.

"I'm called Tandy. Please wait here. I'll get my parents to talk to you."

"We'll go with you," said Sergeant Caputo.

Caputo's grim expression told me that this was not a request. I turned on lights as we headed toward my parents' bedroom suite.

I was climbing the circular stairwell, thinking that my parents were going to kill me for bringing these men upstairs, when suddenly both cops pushed rudely past me. By the time I had reached my parents' room, the overhead light was on and the cops were bending over my parents' bed.

Even with Caputo and Hayes in the way, I could see that my mother and father looked all wrong. Their sheets and blankets were on the floor, and their nightclothes were bunched under their arms, as if they'd tried to take them off. My father's arm looked like it had been twisted out of its socket. My mother was lying facedown across my father's body, and her tongue was sticking out of her mouth. It had turned *black*.

I didn't need a coroner to tell me that they were dead. I knew it just moments after I saw them. Diagnosis certain.

I shrieked and ran toward them, but Hayes stopped me cold. He kept me out of the room, putting his big paws on my shoulders and forcibly walking me backward out to the hallway.

"I'm sorry to do this," he said, then shut the bedroom door in my face.

I didn't try to open it. I just stood there. Motionless. Almost not breathing.

So, you might be wondering why I wasn't bawling, screeching, or passing out from shock and horror. Or why I wasn't running to the bathroom to vomit or curling up in the fetal position, hugging my knees and sobbing. Or doing any of the things that a teenage girl who's just seen her murdered parents' bodies ought to do.

The answer is complicated, but here's the simplest way to say it: I'm not a whole lot like most girls. At least, not from what I can tell. For me, having a meltdown was seriously out of the question.

From the time I was two, when I first started speaking in paragraphs that began with topic sentences, Malcolm and Maud had told me that I was exceptionally smart. Later, they told me that I was analytical and focused, and that my detachment from watery emotion was a superb trait. They said that if I nurtured these qualities, I would achieve or even exceed my extraordinary potential, and this wasn't just a good thing, but a great thing. It was the only thing that mattered, in fact.

It was a challenge, and I had accepted it.

That's why I was more prepared for this catastrophe than most kids my age would be, or maybe *any* kids my age.

Yes, it was true that panic was shooting up and down my spine and zinging out to my fingertips. I was shocked, maybe even terrified. But I quickly tamped down the screaming voice inside my head and collected my wits, along with the few available facts.

One: My parents had died in some unspeakable way.

Two: Someone had known about their deaths and called the police.

Three: Our doors were locked, and there had been no obvious break-in. Aside from me, my brothers Harry and Hugo and my mother's personal assistant, Samantha, were the only ones home.

I went downstairs and got my phone. I called both my uncle Peter and our lawyer, Philippe Montaigne. Then I went to each of my siblings' bedrooms, and to Samantha's, too. And somehow, I told them each the inexpressibly horrible news that our mother and father were dead, and that it was possible they'd been murdered.

Can you imagine the words you'd use, dear reader, to tell your family that your parents had been murdered? I hope so, because I'm not going to be able to share those wretched moments with you right now. We're just getting to know each other, and I take a little bit of time to warm up to people. Can you be patient with me? I promise it'll be worth the wait.

After I'd completed that horrible task—perhaps the worst task of my life—I tried to focus my fractured attention back on Sergeant Capricorn Caputo. He was a rough-looking character, like a bad cop in a black-and-white film from the forties who smoked unfiltered cigarettes, had stained fingers, and was coughing up his lungs on his way to the cemetery.

Caputo looked to be about thirty-five years old. He had one continuous eyebrow, a furry ledge over his stony black eyes. His thin lips were set in a short, hard line. He had rolled up the sleeves of his shiny blue jacket, and I noted a zodiac sign tattooed on his wrist.

He looked like *exactly* the kind of detective I wanted to have working on the case of my murdered parents.

Gnarly and mean.

Detective Hayes was an entirely different cat. He had a basically pleasant, faintly lined face and wore a wedding ring, an NYPD Windbreaker, and steel-tipped boots. He looked sympathetic to us kids, sitting in a stunned semicircle around him. But Detective Hayes wasn't in charge, and he wasn't doing the talking.

Caputo stood with his back to our massive fireplace and coughed into his fist. Then he looked around the living room with his mouth wide open.

He couldn't believe how we lived.

And I can't say I blame him.

He took in the eight-hundred-gallon aquarium coffee table with the four glowing pygmy sharks swimming circles around their bubbler.

His jaw dropped even farther when he saw the life-size merman hanging by its tail from a bloody hook and chain in the ceiling near the staircase.

He sent a glance across the white-lacquered grand piano, which we called "Pegasus" because it looked like it had wings.

And he stared at Robert, who was slumped over in a La-Z-Boy with a can of Bud in one hand and a remote control in the other, just watching the static on his TV screen.

Robert is a remarkable creation. He really is. It's next to impossible to tell that he, his La-Z-Boy, and his very own TV are all part of an incredibly lifelike, technologically advanced sculpture. He was cast from a real person, then rendered in polyvinyl and an auto-body filler composite called Bondo. Robert looks so real, you half expect him to crunch his beer can against his forehead and ask for another cold one.

"What's the point of this thing?" Detective Caputo asked.

"It's an artistic style called hyperrealism," I responded.

"Hyper-real, huh?" Detective Caputo said. "Does that mean 'over-the-top'? Because that's kind of a theme in this family, isn't it?"

No one answered him. To us, this was home.

When Detective Caputo was through taking in the décor, he fixed his eyes on each of us in turn. We just blinked at him. There were no hysterics. In fact, there was no apparent emotion at all.

"Your parents were *murdered*," he said. "Do you get that? What's the matter? No one here loved them?"

We did love them, but it wasn't a simple love. To start with, my parents were complicated: strict, generous, punishing, expansive, withholding. And as a result, we were complicated, too. I knew all of us felt what I was feeling—an internal tsunami of horror and loss and confusion. But we couldn't show it. Not even to save our lives.

Of course, Sergeant Caputo didn't see us as bereaved children going through the worst day of our tender young lives. He saw us as *suspects*, every one of us a "person of interest" in a locked-door double homicide.

He didn't try to hide his judgment, and I couldn't fault his reasoning.

I thought he was right.

My parents' killer was in that room.

READ MORE IN

CONFESSIONS OF A MURDER SUSPECT

NOW AVAILABLE IN PAPERBACK

JAMES PATTERSON
BOOK**SHOTS**

stories at the speed of life

BOOK**SHOTS** are page-turning stories by James Patterson and other writers that can be read in one sitting.

Each and every one is fast-paced, 100% story-driven; a shot of pure entertainment guaranteed to satisfy.

Under 150 pages
Under £3

Available as new, compact paperbacks, ebooks and audio, everywhere books are sold.

For more details, visit: **www.bookshots.com**

BOOK**SHOTS**
THE ULTIMATE FORM OF STORYTELLING.
FROM THE ULTIMATE STORYTELLER.

Also by James Patterson

ALEX CROSS NOVELS

Along Came a Spider • Kiss the Girls • Jack and Jill •
Cat and Mouse • Pop Goes the Weasel • Roses are Red •
Violets are Blue • Four Blind Mice • The Big Bad Wolf •
London Bridges • Mary, Mary • Cross • Double Cross •
Cross Country • Alex Cross's Trial (*with Richard DiLallo*) •
I, Alex Cross • Cross Fire • Kill Alex Cross • Merry
Christmas, Alex Cross • Alex Cross, Run • Cross My
Heart • Hope to Die • Cross Justice • Cross the Line

THE WOMEN'S MURDER CLUB SERIES

1st to Die • 2nd Chance (*with Andrew Gross*) •
3rd Degree (*with Andrew Gross*) • 4th of July (*with Maxine
Paetro*) • The 5th Horseman (*with Maxine Paetro*) • The
6th Target (*with Maxine Paetro*) • 7th Heaven (*with Maxine
Paetro*) • 8th Confession (*with Maxine Paetro*) •
9th Judgement (*with Maxine Paetro*) • 10th Anniversary
(*with Maxine Paetro*) • 11th Hour (*with Maxine Paetro*) •
12th of Never (*with Maxine Paetro*) • Unlucky 13 (*with
Maxine Paetro*) • 14th Deadly Sin (*with Maxine Paetro*) •
15th Affair (*with Maxine Paetro*)

DETECTIVE MICHAEL BENNETT SERIES

Step on a Crack (*with Michael Ledwidge*) •
Run for Your Life (*with Michael Ledwidge*) •
Worst Case (*with Michael Ledwidge*) •
Tick Tock (*with Michael Ledwidge*) •
I, Michael Bennett (*with Michael Ledwidge*) •
Gone (*with Michael Ledwidge*) •
Burn (*with Michael Ledwidge*) •
Alert (*with Michael Ledwidge*) •
Bullseye (*with Michael Ledwidge*)

PRIVATE NOVELS

Private (*with Maxine Paetro*) • Private London (*with Mark Pearson*) • Private Games (*with Mark Sullivan*) • Private: No. 1 Suspect (*with Maxine Paetro*) • Private Berlin (*with Mark Sullivan*) • Private Down Under (*with Michael White*) • Private L.A. (*with Mark Sullivan*) • Private India (*with Ashwin Sanghi*) • Private Vegas (*with Maxine Paetro*) Private Sydney (*with Kathryn Fox*) • Private Paris (*with Mark Sullivan*) • The Games (*with Mark Sullivan*)

NYPD RED SERIES

NYPD Red (*with Marshall Karp*) • NYPD Red 2 (*with Marshall Karp*) • NYPD Red 3 (*with Marshall Karp*) • NYPD Red 4 (*with Marshall Karp*)

STAND-ALONE THRILLERS

The Thomas Berryman Number • Sail (*with Howard Roughan*) • Swimsuit (*with Maxine Paetro*) • Don't Blink (*with Howard Roughan*) • Postcard Killers (*with Liza Marklund*) • Toys (*with Neil McMahon*) • Now You See Her (*with Michael Ledwidge*) • Kill Me If You Can (*with Marshall Karp*) • Guilty Wives (*with David Ellis*) • Zoo (*with Michael Ledwidge*) • Second Honeymoon (*with Howard Roughan*) • Mistress (*with David Ellis*) • Invisible (*with David Ellis*) • Truth or Die (*with Howard Roughan*) • Murder House (*with David Ellis*) • Never Never (*with Candice Fox*) • Woman of God (*with Maxine Paetro*)

NON-FICTION

Torn Apart (*with Hal and Cory Friedman*) • The Murder of King Tut (*with Martin Dugard*)

ROMANCE

Sundays at Tiffany's (*with Gabrielle Charbonnet*) •
The Christmas Wedding (*with Richard DiLallo*) •
First Love (*with Emily Raymond*)

OTHER TITLES

Miracle at Augusta (*with Peter de Jonge*)

FAMILY OF PAGE-TURNERS

MIDDLE SCHOOL BOOKS

The Worst Years of My Life (*with Chris Tebbetts*) • Get Me
Out of Here! (*with Chris Tebbetts*) • My Brother Is a Big,
Fat Liar (*with Lisa Papademetriou*) • How I Survived
Bullies, Broccoli, and Snake Hill (*with Chris Tebbetts*) •
Ultimate Showdown (*with Julia Bergen*) • Save Rafe! (*with
Chris Tebbetts*) • Just My Rotten Luck (*with Chris Tebbetts*)
• Dog's Best Friend (*with Chris Tebbetts*)

I FUNNY SERIES

I Funny (*with Chris Grabenstein*) • I Even
Funnier (*with Chris Grabenstein*) • I Totally
Funniest (*with Chris Grabenstein*) •
I Funny TV (*with Chris Grabenstein*)

TREASURE HUNTERS SERIES

Treasure Hunters (*with Chris Grabenstein*) •
Danger Down the Nile (*with Chris Grabenstein*) •
Secret of the Forbidden City (*with Chris Grabenstein*) •
Peril at the Top of the World (*with Chris Grabenstein*)

HOUSE OF ROBOTS SERIES

House of Robots (*with Chris Grabenstein*) •
Robots Go Wild! (*with Chris Grabenstein*)

OTHER ILLUSTRATED NOVELS

Kenny Wright: Superhero (*with Chris Tebbetts*) •
Homeroom Diaries (*with Lisa Papademetriou*) •
Jacky Ha-Ha (*with Chris Grabenstein*) • Word of
Mouse (*with Chris Grabenstein*)

DANIEL X SERIES

The Dangerous Days of Daniel X (*with Michael Ledwidge*) •
Watch the Skies (*with Ned Rust*) • Demons and
Druids (*with Adam Sadler*) • Game Over (*with Ned Rust*) •
Armageddon (*with Chris Grabenstein*) • Lights Out
(*with Chris Grabenstein*)

GRAPHIC NOVELS

Daniel X: Alien Hunter (*with Leopoldo Gout*) •
Maximum Ride: Manga Vols. 1–9 (*with NaRae Lee*)

For more information about James Patterson's novels, visit
www.jamespatterson.co.uk

Or become a fan on Facebook